LASTING PRIDE

THE PRIDE SERIES

JILL SANDERS

GRAYTON

SUMMARY

Roberta Stanton had grown up a thief on the streets of Portland. Breaking into the old building had been easy, and she'd gotten away with it. Or so she thought. It had cost her the lives of seven close friends.

Years later, Rob finds herself on the other side of the law. Tracking down the thief of millions of dollars' worth of art is the least of her problems. Her dilemma, now, is the handsome owner of that art.

Ric Derby owns the Blue Spot art galleries. Murder and a million-dollar theft bring them together, but a personal vendetta from a dark figure threatens them both. Retreating to the safety of the small town of Pride, Ric must fight to protect the only person he's ever truly loved.

*To my incredible twin,
who has been, and will
always be, with me.*

CHAPTER 1

*S*he could feel her muscles screaming. Her arms shook as she pulled herself up to the window and peeked inside. The shaking had nothing to do with the ninety-degree weather or the fact that she'd strained her tiny arms to pull her ninety-five-pound body up five feet. If someone had asked her, she would have denied that they shook because she was scared. She was a Shadow, and Shadows didn't get scared. No matter what! She peeked into the dark window as she moved her tiny body and got a better hold on the narrow ledge. The old place had sat empty for years; now, however, she could see boxes piled up across the dark room and right in the middle of those boxes sat a small safe. *Bingo.*

Billy would be so proud. He might be a little pissed that she hadn't invited the gang along for the job, but he would overlook it for the loot she was sure to bring back. She knew this old place like the back of her hand; after all, she'd lived in the building for over a year. It was the year right after her old man had ended up dead on the sidewalk outside their hotel room.

She cupped her hands and checked the place out, just to make sure it was empty. She could smell the new paint and noticed that the walls were no longer a dingy brown. Someone had painted them a nice glossy white, making them look new, which actually worked in her favor. Now she would be able to see in the dark better. The light from the streets angled in the tall windows and reflected off the high-gloss walls, illuminating the whole room. She wouldn't even need the penlight that was tucked in her pocket.

Reaching into her other pocket, she pulled out the small knife that her old man had lifted for her tenth birthday. She expertly flipped it open and jammed it under the windowsill, searching for the small lock she knew so well. There! The window creaked then slid open silently. Pulling her agile body over the sill, she slowly slid down to the hardwood floor, listening the whole time and keeping her eyes peeled, just like her old man had taught her.

Hearing and seeing nothing out of sorts, she moved with grace across the floor. Her dirty Keds didn't make a sound on the floorboards. She knew which boards would creek and easily avoided them. Halfway across the room she heard a siren in the distance, and just for a minute, her heart stopped. She stood motionless, waiting, holding her breath, ready to sprint out the window and run for her life. When the sirens started fading, she released her breath in a soft whoosh.

Moving a little faster, she reached the safe. Perfect! It was an older model and she thought she could easily crack this one in her sleep. Leaning over and placing her ear to the cool metal door, she got to work.

It took her almost five minutes to crack the damn thing. She could blame it on the lack of light, but the truth was that her sweaty hands kept slipping on the cool knob. Finally, when the safe door slid silently open, a huge smile appeared on her face. She was seventeen years old and the best thief in Portland, Oregon. Well, she'd been the best ever since her old man had died of a stroke.

Inside the small safe was a treasure. There was over a thousand in cash, which she quickly rolled up and placed in her pocket. There was a large stack of checks, which she left alone. A small black box sat in the back of the safe. Reaching in, she grabbed the silk case and quickly stashed it in her jacket pocket. This was the best haul since she and her old man had broken into the liquor store. She'd been nine at the time and thought they'd hit the jackpot with three thousand dollars. Not to mention her father had grabbed enough liquor to last him a month.

She pulled out the packet of baby wipes from her pocket and wiped the outside of the safe down like she'd been taught, making sure to go over the handle three times. Then she closed the safe with a small click, spun the dial, stuffed the wipes in her jeans, and let herself out of the old building onto Main Street.

An hour later, she made her way over to the base of the Shadows. They weren't the best-known gang in Portland, but they were her family.

As she crawled through the broken fence, Johnny, tonight's lookout, sat on the ground cross-legged, smoking a cigarette.

"Billy's pissed," he said and flicked the butt across the yard.

It was the simple statement that stopped her. She thought of turning around and playing it cool for a couple of days, but instead, she held her chin up and marched in the back door. This week's base was nothing more than an old bowling alley that had half burned down three months ago. No one drove by, and no one bothered them since the neighborhood had gone down the toilet years ago.

She walked into the small room, which hadn't been burned, at the back of the building. She noticed that Bonnie, her best friend, was sprawled across Billy's lap on an old green couch.

The pair had been together since they were six years old after running away from their foster parents. It had taken several years for the relationship to turn from brotherly and sisterly into what it was today. Rob looked up to them and hoped someday to find something close to what they had.

"Where you been, little girl?" Billy asked without taking his eyes off Bonnie. At the sharpness of his voice, Rob cringed. Bonnie sat up and stretched.

"Just strolling," Rob said, dropping the cash on the table in front of the pair. "Thought you might like to eat out tonight." Rob plopped down and sat cross-legged on the floor, leaning against an old leather chair.

"Where did you get this?" Bonnie asked, as she reached over and started to count the money. Billy looked at Rob and, as much as she knew he didn't want to let it show, Rob could tell he was proud.

"Is this how it's going to be? Are you going off on your own all the damn time, not including your family?

4

Damn it, Rob!" He pushed Bonnie off his lap and walked over to pull Rob up by her elbows. "We're a family here, and damn it, if you can't respect that, you can use the door. Got it?"

They were nose to nose now and she could smell the beer. Just for a second, she flashed back to a memory. It wasn't Billy digging his fingers into her skin, but her old man, and this time he wouldn't stop at a simple slap or push. This time it would be bad.

She was shaken out of it when Bonnie said, "Billy, leave her alone!" Bonnie sat down with the cash in her hands. "There's over a thousand here."

Billy turned back to Rob. "Where the hell did you get it?"

"No place just fell from the sky, I guess." Rob took a step forward and challenged Billy. "You want to say otherwise?"

For what seemed like a lifetime, the two battled silently with their eyes. Then Billy blinked and smiled. "Fine, little girl, you have your secrets. Let's go get some grub. I'm starved."

The Shadows consisted of fourteen members and the gang was growing bigger every day. The youngest member was eleven and the oldest was Billy at eighteen.

Rob was second in command, not only because of her age but because of her talent. She was the only member who had received a full education. She'd gone to school and, at fifteen, she had gotten her damn GED. It wasn't as if she was a super genius or anything. She just had a really good memory and picked up on every detail. It wasn't her fault things just stuck. Anyway, her old man had been proud. So proud, in fact, that after she'd received her diploma, he'd taken them out and had gotten wasted. Then he'd robbed a local mart and had beaten the crap out of her a few hours later. Rob didn't want to owe anybody anything and even though the Shadows called her family, she knew exactly what they were.

The three of them made their way over to the local Chuck E. Cheese for some cheese pizzas and root beer. As they walked the few blocks, they ran into other members of the gang. Soon there were eight of them walking along the dark road, and Rob had to admit that she felt more comfortable in the large group.

They were half a block away when she heard the low rumble of the car engine. Looking up, she saw the lights before anyone else did. It seemed like a lifetime, but in reality, it had taken less than a minute for her entire world to change.

CHAPTER 2

*W*hen the cops arrived ten minutes later, there was no one left standing. The ambulance had pulled up a few seconds before the first officer on the scene. The paramedic had just stood and looked in horror.

Bonnie and Billy lay sprawled on each other. Tom and Craig, the two brothers, had tried to run but were now lying face down three feet away. Jenny had been the first to get shot; she had a hole in her head that had turned her pretty blonde hair to a deep red. The other kids looked no better.

"Damn gang wars going on in my fucking backyard." Detective Johns had been on the force for over fifteen years and had never seen anything like what he was looking at. Eight young kids, no older than his own boy, Stephan, had been gunned down half a block from the Chuck E. Cheese, where unknowing families were celebrating birthdays, eating pizza, and playing games.

What was this city coming to? He looked over the faces of the kids and felt his heart break a little.

"Any witnesses?" He already knew the answer but had to ask anyway. Hell, he knew that even if someone had seen what had gone down, no one would step forward.

"No, sir." The young cop, whose face was whiter than a sheet of paper, stepped forward.

"Any IDs?" He knew that answer too. He looked down at a pretty blonde girl and remembered seeing her face on a runaway poster not too long ago.

Just then, he heard a small sound and looked over to a dark-haired girl. Her eyelids fluttered. "Get that goddamn paramedic over here, ASAP! Damn it, man, didn't you check for pulses?" He raced over to the girl and bent to check for one himself. Her pulse was strong, and her skin felt warm. There was blood all over her face, arms, and legs. He ran his hands over her small body, checking for holes. He found none.

"Get your fucking pig hands off me!" It came out as a whisper.

"You just sit still girl, you hear me? Are you shot or hurt anywhere?"

"Get your hands off me," she said again, this time with a little more strength.

"Just hang on here." He shifted so the light fell on the girl's face.

She looked down at her own hands and started frantically trying to rub the blood off onto her jeans.

"Get this off me! Damn it! Get it off me!" She continued to scrub at the blood, using her shirt now. A paramedic handed her a wipe and she went to work trying to clean herself up.

Detective Johns tried to angle her so her back was to the terrible scene. She continued to clean her hands and moved aside as she stood. The paramedics brought a gurney over.

"What's your name?" the paramedic asked while helping her onto the gurney.

"None of your goddamn business," she shot back, still cleaning her hands.

"It would do you a world of good to answer that question," the detective said firmly. The girl looked up at him with large hazel eyes. He could see a small battle in her eyes, and he could see the intelligence radiating from her. This was a smart one, one to be watched, he thought.

She blinked. "Rob...Roberta Stanton."

He smiled. "Well, Roberta Stanton, did you see who did this to your friends?"

The old man wasn't half bad looking, Rob thought. Nice clear blue eyes, wide face, thinning blond hair. Looked like someone else's old man, not hers.

"It was a late model Ford LTD, burgundy, license plate ACF...seven...something." She shook her head. "There were three white guys; the driver was a Hispanic girl about my age. Two had black hoods on, one had a ball cap, and the girl had red streaks in her hair."

"How could you tell all that?" the younger EMT asked while he pulled the blood pressure cuff off her arm. They started to wheel her towards the ambulance.

"Good eyesight and memory, I guess," she shrugged.

"How could you tell they were white if they had hoods on?" Detective Johns asked.

"White hands." She looked over his shoulder to the pile of kids behind him. "They're all dead?" She looked back to him.

"Yes, I'm afraid so. Roberta Stanton...Rob...will you help me get the people who took your family away?"

"They weren't my family," she said, but her eyes told him she was lying.

"Your friends then." He stopped the gurney before the EMTs could put her in the back of the ambulance.

"Yeah, sure. What else have I got to do now?"

Ten years later:

She pulled herself up one last time. Her arms screamed with pain, and her muscles burned from carrying her one hundred-twenty frame. Her eyes were focused straight ahead, not really seeing anything.

"Damn, Rob, how many pull-ups do you do every day?" Rookie Steve Ratter asked from the weight bench next to the chin-up bars.

"One hundred," Sergeant Johns said from behind her.

Breathing outwards slowly, she lowered herself down and wrapped a white towel around her neck. Her arms screamed, her hands ached, and she felt alive. "Nowhere near that many Sergeant, and you know it."

"Rob, I've watched you every day for the past ten years now and know damn well you do one hundred pull-ups every day of your miserable life. Don't be so modest. Rookie"—the Sergeant pointed over to the young man bending over to tie his shoe— "you'd do well to learn discipline from the detective here. She's not only the smartest cop working on the force"—he got a bunch of laughs from the room at that remark— "she's the toughest." The room went silent.

Rob could see the pride showing on the old man's face. It had been ten years since that terrible night her life had changed. The old man had taken her in like she was his own. She'd finished Police Academy in record time, then went on to get her detective badge faster than anyone in Portland's history. She'd taken a year off to do some traveling, thanks to a big bonus she'd gotten one year, but now she had a small apartment on the south side in a nice, quiet neighborhood, a used car that was paid off, and a cat named Jack. She hadn't changed all that much, but one thing was for sure—she was on the right side of the law now. The gold ring on her right finger was a constant reminder of where she had come from.

When she'd gotten to the hospital ten years ago, they had searched her pockets and come up with the black silk box. She hadn't even looked inside it that night, not until Detective Johns had come knocking the next morning. The place she had robbed had reported money missing, but not a ring. They had found the money on Billy and had blamed him. The ring was hers to keep and her burden of the truth.

Now she was the best detective in Portland. She and Detective Johns had taken only two months to track down the killers of the seven kids that night. All four members of the rival gang were now serving life sentences, thanks to her testimony.

She was a little rough around the edges, but she was a cop and felt she had always been destined to be one. Everything leading up to that night ten years ago had prepared her for this life.

"Detective Stanton?" A uniformed officer stood in the doorway.

"Yo," she said, wiping her face with the towel and waving her hand. He walked over and handed her a file for her next case.

Ric Derby had always lived a pampered life. He'd gone to the finest schools his mother's money could buy, he'd driven the fastest cars his father's money could buy, and he'd dated the loosest women, who all wanted his money.

He'd never had to scrape for anything. That was until he decided to go into business for himself. At twenty-two, he'd purchased his first building. Not a house on the upper side, but an old brick building in LA that was half falling down, half burned down. In under a year, the place had been remodeled and opened as his first business. The Blue Spot was more than a gallery; it was a work of art itself, and his only love. He remembered the two years of struggling after he'd opened the place. If it hadn't been for Megan Kimble, now Megan Jordan, he was sure that The Blue Spot wouldn't have been as successful as it was now. With six "Spots" now opened on the West coast, he was even more successful than his parents had been at his age.

His gallery's art ranged from small-time painters to some of the best-known painter/sculptures in modern times. He had over four thousand clients and almost two hundred artists under contract.

It was nine in the morning on a Friday and his place was crowded. Unfortunately, it was black and whites that crowded the old building in Portland, not patrons.

His assistant, Mark Walker, lay face down in a pool of blood. The walls were not blank, as he'd thought they might be. Instead, he noticed only a few places that were now sitting empty.

Had Mark walked in on the burglary? Or had it been an inside job? Mark had only worked for him the last six or so months. Rita, his old assistant, had retired earlier that year. She'd been almost sixty, and in the previous two years, she'd gone from frail to fragile before his eyes. The cancer she'd battled for years would claim her life less than two weeks after her retirement. But now, as Ric looked over at the white sheet that covered his latest assistant, it wasn't the thought of the young man's body that caused his stomach to roll, it was the lost work from the walls. He wasn't coldhearted. In fact, he was deeply saddened by Mark's death. But it was starting to appear that Mark had let the thieves in.

He was standing behind the reception desk giving a uniformed officer his statement when she walked in. The whole room seemed to stop, and everyone turned their heads and watched her glide in. She walked with such fluid motion that his first thought was that she must have been a dancer. She had on dark sunglasses, a dark gray blazer, black slacks that fit just right, and black dusty boots with a slight heel. He could just make out a white shirt under her blazer. No ruffles, no earrings, no jewelry except for a gold ring on her right hand. Her hair was tied back into a long braid that flowed almost all the way down her back. It was black—not just a dark shade of brown, but jet black. She stood at about five-foot-seven, had curves in the right places, and an attitude that demanded respect.

He watched as she moved over to the side of the room where Mark lay sprawled out and then leaned over and quickly removed the sheet.

Ric looked at her face, looking for any signs of emotion. Nothing. She had removed her sunglasses and hadn't even batted an eyelash. He noticed that she took in the whole picture. Removing the sheet completely, she leaned over Mark for several minutes as her partner walked around the room taking notes about the empty spots on the walls. Her partner was a tall blond man who had a young face. He was writing down information from the bronze plates that sat underneath each painting.

"Mr. Derby, it appears that you've been assigned, Detective Stanton. Rob will most likely want to ask you some more questions. Do you have an office?" the officer who had been taking his statement asked him.

"Yes, just up those stairs on the left." Ric looked over at the large blond man. So this was Detective Rob Stanton. All the uniformed cops had been talking about the man all morning. The best detective in Portland, or so they had all said. Ric was really more curious about the man's partner than the tall blond man himself.

Ric headed up the stairs and noticed his office door stood open and the lights were on. No doubt the police had come and gone, searching for suspects or other clues. His office had been gone through, but the safe behind Allison Jordan's *Fairy Queen* painting sat untouched. It appeared the painting had hidden the safe successfully.

His Louis VI desk, however, hadn't fared so well. The chair was smashed and lying in pieces against the east wall. The desk itself was still standing, but there were what appeared to be claw marks on the smooth surface. The drawers had been thrown and pieces were scattered about the room. Taking stock, he noticed that one would have to be rebuilt completely while the other simply needed a little sanding and polish. The easel that sat in the corner or the room, which he used for new art, was a total loss.

He leaned down and pulled out a file that had fallen under his desk.

"I wouldn't touch anything just yet," she said from the doorway.

The man had a nice butt, she noted. She enjoyed the view as he bent down to retrieve a manila folder from under the desk. He wore a suit that looked like it had just come from the cleaners, pressed and starched. Yet to look at his hands and face, one would think that he'd be more comfortable on some beach with a board in one hand and sex wax in the other.

His blond hair was short with a slight wave, and his face and hands were so tanned, one could tell he spent a lot of time outdoors. She could tell the difference between the fake-n-bakes versus a real suntan any day. His was real.

What was this man doing in a suit on Friday morning when the place didn't open until noon? At her voice, he stood up and turned towards her. She pegged him at about six-foot-one, one ninety-eight—a well-defined one ninety-eight. Blond, blue-eyed rich boy who had never seen a day of trouble in his life. She hated him right off the bat.

"I think it might be safe to straighten up a little," he said, setting the folder on the tattered desk.

"If I say leave it, leave it. Are we clear?" Walking behind his desk, she walked right up to the picture and pulled it back, exposing the safe. "Nothing missing from the safe here?" She pulled out a notepad and started writing.

"No, it appears that our thief or thieves didn't know it existed."

"Or they didn't want what was in it." She turned to look at him. "How much money is in there and what documents? I'll need a full report."

"Why do you need to know what wasn't taken?" He asked, leaning against the desk.

"Mr. Derby, if this was an inside job, as I suspect, I'll need to know everything." She pulled one of the black leather chairs upright and took a seat.

"Shall we begin?" She flipped a page on her notepad.

"I was told Detective Stanton would be handling this job? Would you rather wait for him?" He smiled at her.

"I'm Detective Rob Stanton," she said, not looking up from her notepad.

CHAPTER 3

*C*rossing her legs, Rob continued, "My partner has compiled a list of paintings missing from your walls. I'll need a complete inventory of any other items that were taken. I assume you have a storage room?" She looked up.

"Yes, of course, Detective." He crossed his arms and leaned onto the desk. She had hazel eyes. When was the last time he'd seen someone with true hazel eyes? Her lips were unpainted, which of course just drew his eyes to them. She licked them and looked back down at her pad.

"When we are done here, you can show me. Let's start with where you were between the hours of ten o'clock last night and four o'clock this morning."

Two hours later, Ric led Detective Rob Stanton downstairs to his storeroom.

Mark's body had been removed, so all that was left of him was a large bloodstain and white tape marking the spot where his body had lain. At this time, two of his employees had shown up and were being questioned by Detective Stanton's partner.

Julie, his newest employee, was quietly crying into a white tissue provided by the officer.

The storeroom's heavy door had been kicked in and now hung on one hinge. They had dusted it for fingerprints, and he could see the fine powder all over the surface.

As he walked beside the detective, he put a hand on her back, trying to lead her away from the dusty door. She stopped and looked at him, then looked at his hand and raised her eyebrows. He kept his hand in place and smiled back at her. This wasn't a woman who wanted to be led anywhere. He'd seen plenty of independent women in his time, but there was something different behind her eyes. It was almost as if she felt she had to prove herself.

In total, eleven paintings and four sculptures had been stolen. Of those eleven paintings, seven were Allison's.

"Tell me more about Allison Adams," Rob said, walking around the large storeroom. She walked over and placed her hand on the worn windowsill. The window and locks were new but the old wood still showed signs of her life long ago. She ran her hand over the smooth surface and smiled to herself. "You're credited with discovering her, correct?"

"Yes, well it's Allison Jordan now. And Megan Jordan really did the discovering, as you put it. Allison was one of the first local Oregon artists featured here in the Portland Spot."

Rob turned away from the window and walked over to pick up a small painting of a naked man who was half horse, half man. She studied it and placed it back down. "Is her art one of the most expensive that you sell?"

"No, actually. That's the puzzling part. I have paintings that are worth three times what hers go for and those weren't touched. The sculptures were from another local artist, Diego Stephens. Two of his pieces that were taken were fairly new. The other two sculptures were from a well-known artist from Greece." He watched her walk around the room putting notes in her pad. She was efficient; it seemed like nothing she did wasted time.

"Are you in any way romantically linked with any employee or client?" she asked, stopping and looking directly at him.

He smiled a little. "Why Detective Stanton, are you trying to hit on me?" He had hoped to get a flush or a quick denial, but what he got in return was ice. Her eyes went from a warm brandy to a cold hazel in less than a second.

"Mr. Derby, maybe you don't take what you do seriously, but around here"—she paced around the room, and he could tell she was on a roll— "I'm in charge of finding out who murdered one of your employees and stole several thousands of dollars' worth of art. Now, if you—"

"Millions," he interjected.

"Millions, what?" she asked and turned back towards him.

"Millions of dollars' worth of art. Not thousands." He smiled, noting her jaw had dropped a little.

"Mr. Derby, are you telling me that the eleven paintings and four sculptures that were stolen add up to a million dollars?"

"No, Detective." He walked closer to her to get a reaction from her. At least that's what he told himself. He backed her up until she was against the cupboard and countertop. "I'm telling you that several of the paintings and sculptures that were stolen were worth millions. The total for the fifteen pieces stolen would be in the range of $8.3 million. Over $8 million worth of artwork walked out of my gallery last night." He smiled when he got the response he wanted from her. Irritation crossed her face and was quickly replaced with anger. He didn't know why, but that pleased him.

"You want to back off now, Mr. Derby."

"No, I don't think I do, Detective." He reached over her head and flipped open a cupboard behind her. Then he punched in a code on a keypad that sat on the back wall. A hidden door to the right slid open silently.

Rob looked at him and then walked around him into a small dark room. It was no bigger than a broom closet, but it held four large-screen monitors.

"Hiding something are you, Mr. Derby?" She walked over and scanned the screens.

Two of the screens displayed the front gallery; one faced the front door, and the other faced away from the doorway. One screen showed his office and the other showed the back storeroom. She could see the other officers out front, still talking to his staff members.

"No, Detective. I'm just showing the officer in charge what she needs to solve my case. You didn't really think I wouldn't have surveillance on a multi-billion-dollar business, did you?" He smiled again when irritation crossed her face. Why it pleased him so much to see it, he didn't know.

"Can I assume that everything is recorded?" She leaned her hip on the small desk and crossed her arms.

Ric smiled in response.

～

"Detective Stanton, get your skinny butt in my office now!" Sergeant Johns bellowed.

"You did it this time, Stanton." Detective Tom Thomas had been her partner for six years, so she knew when he was joking and when he was serious. This was neither. She got the feeling something was up, but she wasn't quite sure what.

Setting down her pen, she marched into the Sergeant's office, prepared to defend herself no matter what the circumstances were.

"What's up, Sarge?" she asked, walking into the office. Her appearance would have fooled anyone. On the outside, she appeared totally at ease, but inside she felt dread, just as she always did when the Sergeant said those words. Sergeant Mike Johns was more than her commander; he was the father she had always hoped for. He'd actually been like a father to her for ten years now, whether he knew it or not.

"What's up Sarge? What's up Sarge?" he mimicked her. "I'll tell you what's up." He walked over and yanked back the blinds on the windows that faced the bullpen. Rob looked over and saw every officer in her department standing on the other side of the glass. Tom had a large cake in his hands with ten lit candles. Everyone had large smiles on their faces and screamed, "Happy Birthday, Rob."

The sergeant walked over and gave his honorary daughter a kiss on the head and patted her arm.

"What? What is all this?" She stood up straight and looked into his eyes.

"You didn't think we'd forget, did you?"

Rob knew everyone in the whole Portland police department knew where she had come from. It was heart-warming how everyone had pooled together to surprise her, and she felt proud to be part of something so great.

Today wasn't really her birthday. She had never really told anyone her actual birth date and wasn't sure of the date herself. After starting her new life, she'd had to apply for simple things like a social security card and a driver's license. It had taken the sergeant a few months to pull the strings necessary to get new documents for her. None of them were the originals, but it hadn't really mattered to her.

The sergeant had always celebrated her birthday on the anniversary of the shooting. She viewed this as a renewal birthday of some sorts, anyway, so she'd gone along with it.

After all, she'd started fresh ten years ago, and as she looked out at the faces across the glass, she realized she actually felt like part of a family again. Who needed a real family when she had these goofy people who were currently eyeballing the triple-layer chocolate cake like it was a gift sent from the heavens?

"Don't pull this shit on me, sir. You know this is just another of your excuses to eat cake." She saw a smile creep across his face. "Didn't your doctor say you can't eat anything high in sugar?" She walked over and quickly blew out the candles to loud cheers.

22

John's gave her a dirty look and said something even dirtier under his breath. "I guess one small piece won't hurt. That is since it is a special occasion. Ten years of putting up with you, that is." Everyone broke out laughing.

There must be a party going on, Ric thought as he walked into an empty lobby at the police department. He held the DVD copies of his surveillance tapes. Because the feed was live and uploaded via the internet to a security firm in Dallas, he'd had to get them sent overnight. They had been delivered less than a half hour ago, so he figured instead of having them couriered over to the department, he would deliver them himself, so he'd have an excuse to see the detective again.

There was a large woman sitting in the lobby. She was reading a book and didn't even bother to look up when he walked in. A long hall led towards the back of the building, and he saw an older cop walking towards him with a large piece of cake in his hands. Ric met him halfway down the hallway. "I'm looking for Detective Rob Stanton."

The man looked at him and grunted. "Down the hall. Can't-miss her." He continued on his way, eating the cake.

Ric watched the man disappear towards the front, then he turned and walked into a large room. There were desks in rows all over the room, and towards the back, there were a series of glass offices. There must have been about thirty cops standing around, all with their backs towards him, cheering. Then one large cop moved aside and there she was. She was being kissed by an even larger cop. He noticed that she was smiling.

He'd thought she was pretty before, but when she smiled, she was...well...radiant. He smiled in return and he didn't even know why. Just then she looked over and caught sight of him. Her smile disappeared quickly, and the warmth was replaced with ice.

He nodded and kept smiling. He walked towards her and she met him halfway across the room.

"Mr. Derby, how can the Portland Police help you today?" Her voice was smooth and in control.

"Detective." He continued to smile at her. She wore a burgundy short-sleeve shirt today with black slacks that were very appealing. She had boots on again, this time with a little taller heel, and, he noted, silver stud earrings. The gold ring still sat on her right finger.

"Can I help you?" she asked again, this time a little more impatiently.

"Can we talk somewhere?" He nodded, holding up the DVDs.

Rob looked at them. "Sure, follow me." She walked down another hallway and into one of the interrogation rooms that had a TV and DVD player.

"Have you checked these out?" she asked, putting in the first DVD.

"Yes," he said.

She switched the lights lower and pulled up two chairs.

CHAPTER 4

$\mathcal{T}$he surveillance footage was queued to Thursday night at eleven fifteen p.m. She leaned over and hit the start button.

About thirty seconds later, Mark Walker walked in the front door using his keys. Then he reset the alarm and paced the floor for a few minutes. She noticed that he hadn't turned on any lights. The camera must have an infrared night mode.

Then three large men approached the front door and Mark let them in. They stood in the gallery and argued for a few minutes before one of the men—a bald, large man— pulled a gun from his jacket pocket and, to the shock of his companions, shot Mark in the chest. Mark hit the floor— no movement, no twitching, no gasping for a last breath.

The three men argued some more, the bald man waving the gun in the direction of the other two men. Then it appeared they all agreed.

When they got to work, the bald man walked over and

pointed to the pieces he wanted. While his companions, a large Mexican and a thin, dark-haired man, collected the art, he walked to the back room.

He could be seen on the other screen kicking in the storeroom door and, more quickly now, pulling the two pieces that were taken from there. He walked over and placed his palm on the brick wall next to the window. He opened the blinds and stood there for a minute with his hand raised as if he was signaling someone. Then he turned and walked back to the front room where the three men walked up the stairs together. They could be seen on the next camera pulling the desk drawers out of Ric's desk and throwing them across the room. One man slammed the easel against the wall, and the other toppled the chairs.

The bald man sat in Ric's chair and looked through his paperwork. What were they looking for? One of the other men walked over and yanked the fairy picture back and pointed to the safe. The bald man argued with the others for another minute, and they left. The bald one put the fairy painting back in place and walked out. They loaded up the art and closed the door behind them. The room sat dark, with Mark's body lying on the wood floor.

"I think you can file this one as an inside job," Ric said when Rob turned on the lights.

"What were they searching for?" she asked, sitting back down and turning towards him.

She noticed that he was in a dark gray suit today, and he wore his standard blue tie, which was a darker shade of blue today. She had pulled his file, what file there was on the man. It appeared that he was squeaky clean. He ran his business, paid his taxes, dated models or actresses, and had no police record, not even a speeding ticket on file in Oregon or California. Rob didn't like it, or him.

He had come into her office today smiling. She hated it when he smiled. He had perfect teeth, a perfect smile, and a perfect body to go with the package.

"How should I know?" He leaned back in his chair and watched her put on her "cop mask." Her eyes had been raking him up and down and he thought he'd seen a hint of attraction once or twice. But now her face now was blank of emotion, her eyes were cold, and he could just see the wheels turning.

"Do you know any of those men besides Mr. Walker?" She tilted her head slightly.

"No, nor have I seen them in the gallery. I've been spending the last couple of months in my LA offices, and have just recently arrived in town."

"Do you know why they didn't break into your safe?"

"Maybe because it's the latest and best safe on the market?" Ric leaned forward a little.

"Oh, please, I could crack it in under five minutes. Try again." She leaned back and smiled when his eyebrows shot up. "I haven't always been a cop, you know."

"You know, Detective, I believe you *could* open my safe in under five minutes. You asked for a list of items not taken." He pulled out a folder from the briefcase he had set down. "This is a dummy safe. No items of value were in there, and from the looks of the tape, the bald man knew it. How would he know it? Mark Walker didn't even know it. In fact, the only two people who knew it was a dummy safe were me and my old assistant, Rita Barns, who passed away six months ago."

Rob looked over the list he'd given her. One thing you

could say about Ric Derby, he was thorough. Not only did the file consist of a list, but pictures of the paintings and sculptures. There was a neatly typed page titled "items in safe at The Blue Spot, Portland Offices."

"If this is a dummy safe, what is this list?" Rob held up the paper.

"I said that the safe behind the Fairy painting was a dummy safe, that doesn't mean there isn't a real safe in the building." He smiled a little.

"I'm intrigued." She leaned towards him and looked him directly in the eyes. He could tell she was trying to gauge him.

He continued without faltering, a small smile formed on his lips.

"Is it your birthday?" He broke the silence.

She blinked and leaned back. "No." She looked back down at the list.

"Celebrating then?" He noticed her scent, subtle and fresh. He wanted to lean in for a closer smell.

Looking back up, her eyes met his. "It's a pseudo-birthday. I'd like another look at your place," she said, without emotion.

"Can't stand it, can you?" He leaned back now and watched the irritation cross her eyes again.

"What?" She stood and walked over to collect the DVDs.

"Not knowing where the safe is." He also stood and walked closer to her.

"Mr. Derby, this is an official police matter. I would simply like to get more…" She broke off. He was smiling at her. No, he wasn't just smiling, he was grinning like a damn kid, he was having so much fun. "Fine! Yes, it's driving me crazy." She admitted.

"Good, shall we then?" He walked out the door after her.

"I have a few loose ends to tie up here first." She sighed as they looked across the room at the large group of cops still huddled around the quickly disappearing cake.

In a dark car with tinted windows, a dark man sat, waiting and watching.

Not everything had gone according to his plan. That brat Mark Walker had not done his job. He had been assured that everything would be in place, and when it hadn't been, Kenny had taken matters into his own hands. He couldn't blame the man; the plan had been to get rid of the kid all along.

Now he had to rethink everything. He was used to getting what he wanted, whenever he wanted it. He might just have to take matters into his own hands, but he hated getting his hands dirty. Ric Derby had crossed a line and he needed to prove to the man that no one messed with him or his family.

Looking across the street, he watched an old Oldsmobile pull up in front of the brick building. When he saw the woman emerge from the driver's side, he decided it wouldn't be so bad to get his hands dirty after all.

Rob had a large file sitting beside her in her car as she drove to the gallery. Most of it was filled with images and information on Ric Derby. She'd gone through every news article she could get her hands on to learn more about him, and she'd quickly marked him off her main list of suspects. The robbery footage was just the icing on the cake that she needed. Did she think he had anything to do with the theft and murder? No. It was more than her gut that told her that, too. That didn't mean she'd ruled him out completely; his name was still on her backup list.

She couldn't help noticing all the beautiful women he had draped over his arm in most of the photos. It appeared he never held on to them for long, though. The only woman she'd seen him with more than once was Allison Jordan. There had been a dozen or so shots of them clinging to each other. Rob didn't know if he was still in a relationship with the model-beautiful woman now that she was married. The woman was almost the same height as Ric, and blonde and beautiful. The pair looked like a modern-day Ken and Barbie. Jealousy wasn't an emotion she usually felt, and she didn't like feeling the slight twinge she had gotten when she'd looked at the woman on Ric's arm.

She was running late, and she knew she shouldn't have planned to swing by the gallery tonight. But she could never really pass up a challenge, and she saw Mr. Derby as just that.

She'd seen the spark in his eyes—pure, simple attraction. She had never been one to deny herself, as long as it didn't interfere with her job, but Ric Derby would interfere with her current job. She needed to keep her focus on his quaint little shop and not his tight little butt.

When she stepped into the old building, memories flashed like pictures in her mind. She saw herself jimmying the back window open with her pocketknife, bent over the small safe, and curled up sick with the flu in the corner with nothing but a light jacket and a can of beans. This place had too many memories for her liking. She felt a shiver run down her spine. Quickly straightening it, she walked through the doors.

Ric had been watching the detective. Her eyes had been glazed when she had first stepped in, then a shiver ran down her and he could see the "cop mask" being pulled down. Taking his time, he made his way over to where she stood looking at a large portrait painted by another local artist.

"See anything you like?" he asked easily. He noticed she hadn't changed and her shirt now had a dark stain on the front.

She tilted her head to the left a little. "Is this what I think it is?" she asked, looking deeper at the painting.

Ric smiled. "Depends on what you think it is."

She turned away quickly and looked up at him. He had a great smile and she felt herself being pulled in.

"Mr. Derby, you do know that this"—she pointed towards the painting in question— "is illegal in several states, and here you have it up on your walls for everyone to see."

Ric laughed. "Detective, it's just a painting. The viewer sees what they want to see. I see a large maple tree myself. Maybe you should tell me exactly what it is that you see?" He tilted his head to the left a little, mimicking her movements.

"Never mind," she said, quickly moving to the next picture. "You were going to show me around?" she hinted when he laughed at her again. She loathed and liked his smile; he had a carefree way about him. She knew all too well that men like him could get what they wanted when they wanted it, which was all the more reason for her to keep it professional.

"I believe what you wanted to see is back here." He put his hand lightly on her back and walked her towards the stairs.

"I don't believe it." She stood over the hole, looking down at a thing of beauty. "I never thought I would see one of these in my life." She bent down and ran her fingers lightly over the cold metal.

The Brown safe was a thing of wonder. She'd only seen two others in her whole life but had never been able to touch one until now. Looking back up at Ric, she ran her fingers over the metal again.

"May I?"

He smiled. "If you think you can." He stood with his back propped against the bathroom stall. She was just so official, and he could see a blush seeping into her cheeks. He knew she was more excited about his safe than she let on.

He'd done a little research on his detective, and it appears that Roberta Stanton had been a little hell-raiser in her youth. However, on her eighteenth birthday, she'd enrolled in the Portland Police Academy and less than two years later had been promoted to detective, becoming the youngest detective in the history of Oregon.

Now he watched her as she took a deep breath and leaned down to try to break into his safe.

Fifteen minutes later, Ric and Roberta walked out of the men's restroom, laughing.

"That's why I bought a Brown safe." He stopped at the base of the stairs. "And another reason I put it where it is." He smiled at her.

"I can assure you that even with my expertise, I would have never thought to look for that in there." She smiled, enjoying the way he looked a little more relaxed. This was the first time she had seen him so, and it had only added to his appeal.

"If you don't think outside the box, how are you supposed to protect what's yours?"

She got the feeling he was talking about more than his safe when he said that, and wanted to take a step back, but she held her ground.

"Would you care for some tea?" He nodded towards his office.

Looking down at her watch she said, "I can't, actually, I'm already late." She took a step backward. "Thank you for showing me, well, everything." She smiled and backed away further.

"How about lunch?" he asked casually.

She stopped and looked at him, hard. He looked relaxed, standing in the lobby of his multimillion-dollar art store and he was asking an ex-thief out. Did he know? Would he care?

"Can't, you're a case. See you later." She didn't give

him a chance to reply as she quickly walked out. She needed to get out of there, away from his infectious smile.

He enjoyed watching her walk out of his place. The woman kept amazing him. He enjoyed discovering new things about her each time they met. And he was looking forward to learning even more.

CHAPTER 5

*Y*ou can think of a lot of crazy things when you're flying through the air upside down. At times like this, Rob always seemed to think of grocery lists or paperwork she had forgotten to file. Her mind always cleared up, though, after hitting the mat, when the wind was knocked out of her temporarily.

She loved it. Looking up and over, she could see the smile on Craig's face. He must have lost a tooth since last week. Now his smile was not only shockingly handsome, it was downright cute.

Better not mention that to him, though. Rob knew that even though he was only ten, he'd had a crush on her for the last year. And any mention of it caused the skinny ten-year-old to break out in a beet-red blush that covered his face and neck.

"Have you been working out, Craig?" Rob pulled herself up from the mat. "I swear I'm going to have to start asking you to pull some of your energy back, so I don't get thrown through the wall." The pair bowed, and Craig giggled.

Rob had been teaching at Mr. K's for almost eight years now. She had attended classes for two years, and then after receiving her fourth black belt, she had decided to try her hand at teaching. She ended up being one of the top teachers at the large studio.

Now there were people who changed their schedules to Tuesday or Thursday evenings just to attend her classes. She still did one-on-one training with several of the younger kids from troubled homes once a week. She made sure that Mr. K didn't charge for those classes. She also did several special classes each year for self-defense for women. That was one of her more popular classes and was usually booked solid.

"Shall we try that again?" she asked, circling around the young boy with a huge grin on her face that matched his.

It was one of those days Ric would have rather avoided. After spending two hours on the phone with one of his art dealers, he wanted to throw something against the wall. He paced up and down his small office and swore he would never deal with the Indian Government again. They were one of the worst embassies to deal with, at least when it came to their artists. The Egyptians, Chinese, and even the Russians had nothing on them. They were not eager to export their art, especially when it came to their new artist, who just happened to be a woman on top of it all.

~

Tossing down the file he had on Sannidhi Rangan, or Sandi as she prefers to be called by the Americans, he felt even more disgusted at them for holding women back, culturally. Not only was Sandi's art being held by the country— for religious reasons, they claimed—but now it appeared that the seventeen-year-old girl was nowhere to be found.

He opened the file and looked at the young girl's face. All he could see from beneath her hijab where her dark eyes, but he could see deep desires within them. The dull colors of the garment did little to extinguish the flames in the young girl's eyes. Her art had been something Ric had immediately desired. He knew it was not only one of a kind but something that would eventually become an enormous asset to both him and the young woman who'd created it.

Usually, he didn't deal with artists so far away. But when an old friend had pulled him aside at his last art show in London, he'd taken one look at the piece he'd brought with him and had wanted to sign her on immediately. He'd talked to the girl only once when he'd made arrangements for her to fly out to New York for a meeting. She'd never gotten on the flight and he hadn't heard from her since then.

Ric stormed out of his office and headed downstairs to talk to Kimberly, his new, temporary assistant. He didn't have any time to go looking for a permanent assistant just now. He had a stack of resumes to choose from—they took up an entire corner of his desk—but knowing he had to find someone by the end of the month caused him even more stress.

When he walked down the wide staircase that sat along the brick wall in his main gallery, Ric noticed a tall, dark-haired man hovering over Kimberly. He could tell by the young girl's face that she was transfixed and thoroughly enjoying the conversation.

Speeding his steps, he reached the pair and vaguely overheard part of the conversation.

"Of course not, Mr. Cardone. I don't mind giving you a call," Kimberly said, almost purring the remark. She looked over as Ric approached.

When the man turned around, Ric guessed that he was a few years younger than he was. Where Ric's features were light, marking his father's Scandinavian heritage, this man was almost his complete opposite. Ric had a dark tan from hours of running along the beach in the California sun, but this man's skin was dark due to his Mediterranean heritage. That would also account for the thickness of his accent. His black hair was slicked back, and his dark eyes ran up and down Ric as if he were weighing his options.

Then he extended a hand and said, "Mr. Derby, I'm Dante Cardone. I've been doing business with you for several years now."

Ric remembered the name. He'd never seen the man in person, though; he usually attended auctions over the phone or computer. Never in the three years, he'd worked with him had he seen a picture of him, let alone seen him face to face.

"Mr. Cardone." He shook the man's hand.

Ric noticed the dark gray suit for what it was— expensive. There was a large gold ring he wore on his left hand with a rather unique and old design. He saw that, too, for what it was—heritage.

"How can I be of service to you today?"

There was something in the way the man looked at him that caused Ric to maintain his stance. He didn't like the almost sneer that had crossed his face as he spoke.

"Mr. Derby, I'd like to inquire about a piece that your lovely assistant here"—he looked back at Kimberly and winked at her— "says was shipped over a week ago, but has yet to arrive."

"I apologize for any misunderstanding." Ric walked behind the counter to look at the invoices Kimberly was holding. "It does appear that we've already shipped you this item." Ric watched anger fly into the man's face so quickly that Kimberly, who'd been happy to flirt with him up until now, quickly took a step back.

"Well, since I'm currently standing in your gallery, I can assure you I have yet to receive what I've paid for." Ric could almost hear the grinding of his teeth.

"I would be happy to check with our shipping company. It may take a day or two to figure this out. I assure you, Mr. Cardone, I will get to the bottom of this matter, personally."

Seven hours later, when Ric walked into the apartment he kept in Portland, he had a huge headache. The last thing he wanted to hear was his sister's voice on the answering machine.

"Hi Ric, it's me, Katie. Of course, you know it's me. Who else would be calling you on your personal line? Surely not a girlfriend, since you never keep a woman for too long. Anyway, I was just calling to tell you Mom and Dad are finally getting a divorce. Yup," his sister sighed,

"Mom's in Rome or Venice, or somewhere where the men are tall, dark, and half-naked, and Dad is fishing in Alaska. Soooo, I thought you might want to call them and work your magic. Oh, by the way, I'm getting married. Well, at least I've found the man I want to marry. He doesn't know it yet, but anyway…I guess I'll talk to you later. I think I've talked long enough that your machine—"

His answering machine beeped with the end of the message. He smiled when he heard the next message.

"…is going to cut me off. Love you, big brother."

Katie was Ric's complete opposite in every sense. His sister was as whimsical as he was organized and orderly. Where Ric was blond and blue-eyed, like their father, Katie had dark curly hair and chocolate caramel eyes. She was almost eleven years younger than him and to his knowledge was still attending college back east. This was the fourth time since starting college that she'd told him she was getting married.

He thought she was in love with being in love, something he'd never experienced before. Oh, he'd felt a distinct like, a bout of infatuation, and a good dose of old-fashioned lust. But never love. It wasn't that he was incapable of love. After all, he loved his sister and he felt love for Allison Jordan and a few others, in the same way. His parents, he tolerated.

As for his parents getting a divorce, it seemed like every other month they were getting one. His mother took off to Rome or some other place where the men were tall, dark, and half-naked, as his sister had said, at least once a year. As for his father's fishing trips, well, he thought he knew why he was going to Alaska once a year, lately. And he was sure the hot little redhead didn't have fishing on her mind. Maybe this was why Ric never put himself out there?

But this was the way his parents worked. Ever since Ric could remember, he'd been patching their relationship.

The last message that played on his machine took his mind off his family issues completely.

"Mr. Derby." Her voice was even sexier on his machine. He walked over and stood right in front of the large windows that overlooked Mount Hood and the Columbia River and listened. "This is Detective Stanton. I have some information I'd like to go over with you. Please return my call at your convenience." When his machine clicked at the end of the message, he smiled.

Picking up his phone, he punched her number.

"Detective Stanton, this is Mr. Derby returning your call. When you get this message, please return my call at *your* convenience."

Wishing he could be there to see the irritation cross her face, he then punched his mother's number into the phone and started "working his magic," trying to mend his dysfunctional family.

The next morning as Rob sat in the bullpen, she listened to her messages and laughed. How did that man know how to irritate her so much? But she was in a good mood today and wouldn't let a call from a very handsome, but irritating, Ric Derby hinder it.

Just as she was going to pick up her phone to call him back, Brian, a new detective, walked up to her and leaned on her desk.

"So," he said, letting his eyes wander over her gray blouse, "I hear we caught your art thief." He continued to stare at her chest instead of her eyes.

"Brian," Rob said, in a very calm voice, "if you don't get your sleazy ass off my desk and your beady little eyes off my chest"—she smiled up at him— "I'm going to take my stun gun out and stick it between your legs." She stood and walked to the sergeant's office without looking back, but from the sounds behind her, she knew he'd removed his butt from her desk.

"Why did I have to hear about you guys catching my art thief from tall, sleazy, and annoying out there?" She nodded towards the large windows that overlooked the bullpen as she stood in the sergeant's office.

"Because you were late," he said, without looking up from the pile of paperwork on his desk.

"Bullsh—" She didn't get to finish since he'd raised his head and was giving her a death stare. She cleared her throat. "That's bull and you know it, sir." She sat down on the couch. He had two perfectly good black leather chairs right in front of his desk that everyone else always sat on. Rob, however, chose to sit further back in the room on the soft couch. Crossing her legs, she continued, "I'm never late."

Smiling, the sergeant stood up and walked around his desk then leaned a hip on the corner.

"Do you know why I took this job?" he asked.

Rob had played this game with him several times over the past five years since he'd been promoted to sergeant.

"No sir, tell me why." She smiled at his irritation.

"No sir, tell me why," he mimicked with a smile on his face. "You know damn well why I took this job. I took this job, so I wouldn't have to deal with snot-nosed punks like you." His eyes laughed as he crossed his arms over his chest.

"Now you have to deal with all that." She pointed to the large pile of papers that covered half of his desk.

He took a big breath and released it. "Your bald art thief is in holding room five. They brought him in at"—he leaned over and pulled a file from a stack— "zero six hundred hours. He was getting gas at a 7-Eleven when one of our black and whites spotted him. The arrest was quiet. Kenny Sorvillo—that's your perp—called his lawyer, a Mr...." He flipped the file open and pulled out a business card and handed it to her.

"Mr. Kent," she read out loud.

"Like I said, *they* are in room five. Go get 'em." He tossed her the file.

Two hours later, Rob had sweat trickling down her back and a growing headache. It appeared that Mr. Kent knew what he was doing. Not only did his client obey his every eye twitch, his lawyer was pulling the whole *"you've got the wrong man"* scenario. And his lawyer had some shady proof to boot. Rob didn't like it. Something about the whole setup stunk. But since his lawyer had a hotel receipt that put Kenny Sorvillo in Kalama, Washington—a good forty-minute drive from The Blue Spot—on the evening of the burglary, they could only hold him until a judge looked at everything and set bail, which might happen later that day.

But the icing on the cake of proof had been the late-night purchase at a local diner, which showed that Mr. Sorvillo had not only spent the night in Kalama, but he'd enjoyed a midnight snack, complete with a receipt and his signature.

The man might even walk free if the judge allowed. But that didn't mean he had to walk far and without someone watching him.

CHAPTER 6

*R*ic was busy looking over his files as the plane landed in LA for a charity show that night. He had been planning it for months. The event was for another Alzheimer's charity that Allison had gotten him involved in a few years back when her mother had been diagnosed, and she had several new pieces in tonight's auction. Since it was hosted at his gallery, he had personally made sure that everything was in place.

He enjoyed charity events more than the normal art events that came with the job. Stuffy people in stuffy rooms. And since this one was in his own place, he was a lot happier to attend it.

He usually spent a few months in California a year, but for the most part, he'd taken to running everything from his Portland offices. He felt more at home there and had begun to consider it the base of his operation.

Later that evening as he stood next to Countess Regina, one of his regular patrons, he watched his friend Mitchell Kovich march across the room, heading in his direction.

Mitchell was his contact in New York, the man who'd introduced him to Sandi.

"There you are, Ric," Mitchell said, pulling a flute of champagne off a waiter's silver tray as he passed. "I've been trying to get a hold of you the last few days."

Ric excused himself from the countess and pulled Mitchell across the room where there were fewer people. His friend was several years younger than he was and had the wiry frame of a swimmer. Swimming is what had brought the two together in college. Mitchell had been a skinny freshman being picked on by some of the larger swim team members. Ric had been walking by and had stopped the fight. Mitch had a broken nose and a new friend to show for the incident.

"What the devil is going on with Sandi? I haven't been able to get through to her for weeks. The embassy is a mess—"

"Hang on there, Ric, I've some news on that subject." He took a large swig of his drink and grabbed another from the same waiter, who'd circled the room. Ric started getting concerned since he knew Mitch wasn't a drinker. "There's been a major…incident."

"Incident?"

"Listen, Ric"—Mitch looked around the room— "things have gotten a little out of hand." He tossed back the next drink. "I've had to pull some strings, using your name, and I think I screwed up big time."

"What do you—" Just then, Ric's cell phone vibrated. Looking at the number, he recognized the detective's office number. "Hang on, I've got to take this call."

Ric answered as he watched Mitchell walk back across the room and grab another flute, which he downed quickly.

His friend kept looking around the room, looking for someone, or looking to avoid someone he didn't know.

"How can I help you this evening, Detective?" he said smoothly.

"You can tell me where the hell you are and why your butt is not in Portland." He could hear the anger in her voice. "Why didn't you tell me you were leaving town? We have an open case here, and you go flying off to be with…" He heard her take a deep breath.

"I wasn't aware that the Portland PD needed to know my whereabouts at all times." He leaned against the door jam and enjoyed the annoyance in her voice. Would her eyes be sparking fire as he imagined? He smiled, imagining the flames shooting in his direction.

"Listen, Mr. Derby, I need to know if you leave town for any length of time. I'm trying to run an investigation here unless you forgot."

"How could I forget? After all, it is my art that is missing, and my assistant that was killed." He could hear a loud noise on her line in the background.

"Yeah, well—" He heard her drop the phone, then there was a loud popping noise and finally he heard her say, "Someone come get this damn drunk off the floor, he just puked all over my boots." After a shuffle, she said, "Brian, you jackass, next time cuff the perp before you decide to take a bathroom break. He not only puked on my new boots, he's also torn my good shirt. You owe me big time, rookie."

He didn't hear the man's reply, but when Rob came back on the phone, he thought she said, "Asshole," under her breath.

"Problem, Detective?" Ric asked.

"Nothing that 50,000 volts and a good shoe shine couldn't handle." He chuckled as she continued. "Listen, I need to know when you leave Portland. I've got some questions—"

"I'll be back in town tomorrow midday. How about we meet for lunch?"

"No, I'll stop by later this week." He thought he heard annoyance in her voice as she hung up.

Ric hung up with Rob and looked around for Mitchell, but he was gone. His behavior was making Ric uneasy. Sandi had disappeared and now Mitch was acting nervous, which wasn't like him. Ric knew he had some things to check into when he got back to Portland

Rob hung up the phone and looked down at her torn shirt and her freshly puked-on boots.

Her annoyance wasn't with the boots or her clothes; Ric Derby was the cause of her problems right now. The man had flown to LA today without telling her he was leaving town. She'd called his office and his assistant had informed her that he was out of town for a show with Allison. It wasn't as if she needed to keep an eye on him, but he was a suspect, even if he was very low on her list. Okay, dead last on her list. But he was still on it.

She marched out of the office to clean up her shoes and put on the backup shirt she kept in her locker.

Ric Derby was trouble. She knew it, so why did she have to find his voice so damn sexy?

The next evening Rob sat at her desk nursing a bad mood brought on by Brian harassing her all day. When she looked up and saw Ric walking across the crowded room, she immediately went on alert.

Why did he have to look so good? His suit was dark gray this time. Did he have a full closet of them in different colors? He had his standard bright blue tie on again, which matched his eyes perfectly. Did he have them specially made? Here it was seven o'clock in the evening, and he looked like he'd just walked off the catwalk.

Waving at him, she nodded as he approached.

"I thought we decided I'd stop by later this week." She went back to the stack of papers on her desk, giving each her full attention. Well, maybe not her fullest. How could she concentrate when he was staring at her like that?

"You agreed." He sat in the chair next to her desk. "I, on the other hand, didn't say anything of the sort." He leaned closer to look at the papers she was trying to concentrate on. "You look busy."

"Hmm." She flipped the page. "I'm searching through your records, trying to find a connection between the pieces taken."

Well, why don't we take these someplace quieter and grab some food while we're at it? I'd be glad to help out." He started to pick up one of the large stacks of files she had.

"No," she said, trying to stop him. "I can handle my job just fine." He sat the files back down.

"Just trying to help. After all, this was my art. I do have a little more background on them than these files would provide." He smiled.

Looking at him, she tilted her head and realized it was true. He'd know the artists personally and he probably even knew what they were wearing when each one was painted.

"Fine, but you're paying for dinner."

The dark man watched as the couple left the building together. He'd followed her back over to the police station, trying to find a pattern, trying to find his opening. He wanted his hands on the woman. After seeing her for the first time, he knew she was another item he wanted. Nothing had ever stopped him before, and he always got what he wanted. But he had Ric to take care of first before he could think about his own pleasures.

He would just have to change his plans a little. Move his pawns around and find his best strategy. He was good at strategy; after all, that's what people paid him loads of money for.

"You've got someplace here. Nice view." She walked around his apartment, looking out at the lights of the city, which reflected off the river.

He liked the tight black pants she wore. They had pockets with buttons on her butt, which just made him want to look at her butt more. She'd removed her jacket and he admired the button-up short-sleeved shirt she was wearing. The dark red color set off the tones of her hair.

"It has its perks." He set the large box of files on his coffee table. The pizza box was balanced on top of it. "Do you want some wine with the pizza?" He walked to the kitchen, and she followed.

When he opened the refrigerator and pulled out a beer, she said, "I'll take one of those."

Two hours later, the stack of files was spread out all over his coffee table and the floor—financial papers in one pile, buyer history in another. There didn't seem to be any connection between the pieces. At least, none that they could tell.

She sat back and rubbed the back of her neck. He could see the tension in her face when he'd arrived at her desk. She'd looked annoyed at his arrival. He enjoyed riling her but knew that he would cross the line if he did it when she was hurting.

They sat side by side on the couch, and when he started to pull her towards him, she tensed.

"I'm just going to help you out, trust me." She looked at him for a minute, gauging him. Then he could see the decision in her eyes. She allowed him to pull her closer, and when he turned her around, he started massaging her shoulders. He could feel the tension dissolving under his fingers. She moaned a little and leaned her head forward, giving him full access to her neck and shoulders. Gently he moved her French braid over her shoulder and continued moving his hands over her slender form.

"I can't quite figure you out."

"What's there to figure out? You probably know more about me than I do. I bet you have a file twice as thick as these on me, somewhere."

"Hmm, yes," she admitted. "But it didn't cover this."

"What?" He was completely focused on the skin just

under her ear. He bet it was soft and tasted of honey. Would she moan if he kissed her there?

She turned around and looked at him. He'd removed his tie and jacket, had unbuttoned his sleeves and had rolled them up. He looked and felt at home.

"You're quite the charmer. I get that you have a stake in finding your missing art. But why are you helping me out tonight? I mean, most people would cringe at the thought of getting their hands dirty in a stack of paperwork like this." She waved her hand over the disarray of papers lying all over his living room.

"Well, my intention, when I walked into your office, wasn't to do paperwork." He tried for casual.

"Then what were they?"

"To see you. But by helping you out with this paperwork, it allowed us to go on our first date." He smiled.

"This is not a first date." She looked taken aback.

He thought about it a minute. "You know, you're absolutely right." He leaned forward and brushed his lips gently over hers before she could move away.

Her lips were soft and warm, and he could taste the pizza sauce, beer, and her. He ran a hand up her neck and gently cupped the back of her head to hold her to him, his hand resting just on her neck. She'd leaned into him and he felt her hand on his leg, holding her upright.

He pulled back and looked into her eyes. They reminded him of the color of his morning cappuccino. He could see that they were unfocused and confused.

"There, now we can call it a date." He went to lean closer and kiss her again, but she held up a hand to his chest.

"I—I can't get involved. You're part of an ongoing

investigation, and—" He took her mouth again, this time with a little more pressure.

Her hand was trapped between them, and she held onto his shirtfront, holding him close. He ran his fingers into her loose braid and enjoyed the softness of her hair. She had an intoxicating taste and he marveled at the differences he was now feeling in her.

Gone was the tough cop with a hard exterior shell. She'd been replaced by a soft, very sexual woman who was melting under his light touch.

Her tongue darted out to play across his lips and he enjoyed the moment, exploring her soft mouth and the zesty mixture of beer and pizza on her tongue.

Pulling her closer, he realized she was almost in his lap. He ran his hands over her, enjoying the softness of her curves, the length of her legs and arms. She wrapped herself around him as he pulled her up onto his lap so that she was straddling him. She rubbed herself against his pants where it was obvious what she was doing to him.

This only caused him to get harder as she rubbed lightly against him. His eyes almost crossed when her hips started moving, riding him faster. He enjoyed the feel of the clothes between them and wondered if she enjoyed it as much as he did.

He grabbed her hips and held on when he felt her melt against him. Her hands were fisted in his hair. She'd taken complete control and he was enjoying every minute.

He ran his hands up under her shirt and cupped her. She was warm and soft, and he played with the silk she wore until he could feel her nipples pushing against his fingers. Then he leaned back and flipped open a couple buttons to expose the black, silky bra.

She rolled her head back and moaned, holding his head to her.

Leaning in, he ran his mouth over the column of her neck, enjoying the spicy taste and smell of her, until finally, he pulled the silk aside and took her nipple into his mouth, sucking lightly.

Just then her cell phone rang from across the room, and they jumped away from each other as if they were teenagers caught making out on the couch.

Standing up quickly, she walked over to her jacket and pulled the phone out, answering it while she tried to button and tuck in her shirt.

"Detective Stanton." She paused. "How long ago?" She looked over at Ric. He continued to sit there with the proof of his desire tenting the front of his pants. "Yeah, I'll be there in twenty." She hung up as she finished tucking in her shirt, then she threw her jacket on and started piling the papers back in the box.

"Well, this was…" She finished putting all the files back in the box and looked up at him.

"Don't." He crossed the room to take her shoulders in his hands. "Don't belittle it by saying 'it's been fun, see you around.'" He bent and kissed her again, sparking the flames he knew she felt, as well.

"Go." He pushed her lightly towards the door. "Be a cop. But remember that I want you, want this. Until next time."

She walked out, carrying the boxes under her arms. Her hair was a mess, her shirt was untucked in the back, and he knew she was as affected as he was.

CHAPTER 7

*R*ic couldn't sit still any longer. He shoved his chair back and paced the room. He had spent over an hour trying to track down Dante Cardone's art, and all he'd hit was a brick wall. The art had been delivered to the man's business, according to Jordan Shipping, which had faxed him a signed copy of the delivery order. But it had been signed by none other than Mark Walker. What had his assistant been doing across town at Mr. Cardone's business? Why had he signed for the piece?

He was now on his fifth call to Mr. Cardone's offices and was still on hold waiting for the man to answer his phone.

Ric knew that he was a busy man, but it usually took someone only a few minutes to answer a call.

What did Dante Cardone do that he couldn't answer a simple phone call? Especially one he was waiting for.

Just then he looked up and noticed the detective standing in his doorway. He motioned her in just as Mr. Cardone' secretary came back on the line.

"Mr. Cardone will take your call now." There was a click.

"Dante Cardone."

Ric watched Roberta step in and sit comfortably in one of his chairs.

"Mr. Cardone, Ric Derby here. I've got some more information about your delivery. Will you be available for a meeting with me and the police in say"—he looked at Rob, who looked confused— "an hour?"

"Yes, Mr. Derby, I can clear my schedule. Do you know where we're located?"

"Yes, we can find your building. We'll see you then. Goodbye." He hung up quickly.

"What was that all about?" Rob asked, crossing her legs. He noted how good they looked in the tight-fitting, dark khaki pants.

Walking over, he handed her the file. "What do you make of this?"

She looked over the paperwork he'd been staring at the last half an hour while waiting to have his brief conversation with Dante Cardone.

"Hmm," she said, with her head down. He noticed the way the lights shined off the rich darkness of her hair. She'd worn it loose today, and it hung straight down her back with a slight curl. "I'd say it's worth talking to Mr. Cardone. And since you've efficiently made plans for us through my lunch break, you can buy me lunch," she said, standing up and handed the file back to him.

He smiled at her and they walked out of the room together.

This wasn't the kind of place Rob thought he'd take her to eat. The greasy burger place was one that she frequented and was actually one of her favorite places to eat. It was also run by two of her favorite people.

~

Kenny, the owner, and head cook, stood just behind the counter. His red hair was tied back with a net, and his face matched the color of his hair.

"Well, lookie what we got here. Ric, what're you doing with my Rob?" the three-hundred-pound man said, pointing his spatula at the pair.

"Your Rob?" Ric asked the man and leaned against the countertop. "Kenny, I wasn't aware you owned another woman. Does Barbara know about this?" he asked, joking about the man's wife, who stood a few tables away helping other customers.

The large, chocolate-skinned woman walked up and bumped him on the hip, smiling at him. "If he gets to own her," she said, nodding towards Rob, who had seated herself on the stool next to Ric, "then I get dibs on you, sweetie." She reached up and pinched his cheek then smiled at the pair.

"What'll you two have?" she asked, walking around the counter.

"I'll take my usual." He looked at Rob, waiting for her to order.

"Me too. This time Kenny, can you add some extra fries on it since I've got class tonight. I've been trying to beat Tommy. I swear that kid of yours has packed on a few pounds since last month." She smiled at the couple and leaned over the counter to grab herself a bottled water, then leaned over again and tossed one to Ric.

"How long have you been eating at Barb's?"

Ric laughed. "Well, let's see. I met Barbara a few years back when she came in and wanted to 'fancy up the joint.' Her words, not mine. Then she got me hooked on their turkey burger and I've been coming here ever since. You?"

She chuckled. "Turkey burger, eh? I figured you for a turkey burger kind of guy. I've known Kenny since I was twelve when he caught me stealing from his register. He's been feeding me greasy burgers ever since."

"Why do I get the impression you had an interesting childhood?" He watched her start to twist the paper napkin in her hand. When she noticed, she set it down and straightened her black shirt.

"Tell me about Dante Cardone." She changed the subject so quickly, he laughed.

Forty minutes later, Ric walked into the Cardone's business building, whistling. Rob tilted her head and looked at him.

"Nice digs," he murmured as they walked through the large marble lobby of the building, causing her to chuckle.

They looked at the directory and found the floor they wanted, which was near the top. Taking the elevator, they rode up in silence. Ric watched her as the elevator doors slid closed. He'd seen the way she had shifted gears at the diner. She'd become more open and friendly, and she'd remained so on the short drive downtown. Now, however, he could see that she was starting to put on her "cop mask" and he liked seeing the small changes in her. She stood up straighter and carried her back and shoulders differently. Her eyes were not as soft as they'd been when she'd been talking to her friends. Now she carried herself with an air of command.

Roberta's mind and eyes caught everything, such as the way Ric had been warm and relaxed around her friends. She had actually enjoyed his company over the short lunch break. He had watched her in the elevator; she wondered why he'd stared at her so intently. It was almost as if he were trying to solve a puzzle. She was no puzzle. Sure, she had her little secrets. She liked her little secrets. But for the most part, she was an open book. Most everyone she worked with knew her whole life story. After all, most had been there when she'd been on the other side of the law. The newbies and rookies quickly learned her history, and then she'd teach them to fall in line and they'd give her respect and space.

As they walked into the plush uptown office, the first thing Rob noticed about Dante Cardone was how much he reminded her of Ric. There were more differences than similarities—where Ric was blond, blue-eyed, and fair-skinned, Dante had jet-black hair and dark chocolate eyes, and his skin showed signs of a Mediterranean heritage—but she could see the same underlying bone structure in their faces and noticed that they were roughly the same height and build.

She also noticed the change in Dante's face when he watched her walk in beside Ric. She could tell that he was a womanizer from the second she laid eyes on him. When he saw her, his whole persona changed, he became smoother and smiled a little more.

"Hello, Mr. Derby." He shook Ric's outstretched hand.

"Mr. Cardone, this is Detective Roberta Stanton. She's in charge of the investigation into some missing art and the death of my assistant Mark."

"Please," he motioned to two chairs. When they sat, he continued. "How can I help you both today?"

"As you know, I did some research into your missing artwork, *The Indian*." Setting the file on the desk, he pushed it towards Dante and waited for the man to open it. "The shipping receipt from Jordan Shipping shows a signature"—Ric pointed to it— "from Mark Walker, who was employed up until last week at my gallery as my personal assistant. So, the question seems to be, why did Mark sign the receiving paperwork for your artwork?"

"This is a mystery. I'd never heard of Mark Walker. At least not until I read what had happened down at your shop in the local news." He looked at Rob. She could tell that he wasn't really seeing her but looking through her as he thought. Then, without a word, he picked up his phone.

"Stacey, would you come in here, please?" A few seconds later, a tall, blonde woman walked in. Rob didn't know how women walked in heels like that. They had to be four inches of pain. But the woman walked gracefully over to her boss.

"How can I help you, Mr. Cardone?"

"Stacey, this is Mr. Derby and Detective Stanton. Can you do an employee search on a Mark Walker? Please see if he has ever been employed either by me or my father. You can get back with me and pass on your findings to both the detective and Mr. Derby." He handed her the file.

"Yes, of course. I'll get this information to you soon." When she walked out of the room, Ric stood up to leave.

"I have a few questions for you, Mr. Cardone." Rob took out the small pad and pen she always kept in her jacket.

Half an hour later, Ric and Roberta rode the elevator down to the parking garage.

He really liked it when she played cop, especially with someone like Cardone. She'd maintained the cop persona until the elevator doors had shut. Then he watched as she relaxed against the wall. She slowed her breathing down and her eyes softened. He was so turned on by her.

Walking across the empty compartment, he stopped right in front of her, his hands on either side of her on the railing. He saw her eyes heat just before his mouth claimed hers.

When the doors opened, her hair was a mess and her lips were slightly swollen. His nicely pressed shirt was now untucked and a little crooked and they both had large smiles on their faces.

"Well, that was a perfectly good waste of an afternoon. How can that man run a multimillion dollar company and not know the answers to some of my very basic questions."

Ric laughed as he opened the car door for her. She stopped and looked at him. "You know, if I didn't know any better, I'd say the two of you were brothers." Ric stopped laughing and his head tilted to the side as he thought about her statement.

She slid into his car and waited for him to close the door. When he just continued to stand outside the open door, staring into space, she got back out and looked at him.

"Hey, are you okay?" She placed a hand on his arm.

He blinked and looked at her. "You know, I thought there was something about him. I wonder…"

"Ric?"

He looked at her, and she realized he was standing so close that she could see the different shades of blue in his eyes.

Without saying anything, he reached up and brushed aside a strand of her hair that had fallen forward.

"Ric?" It was more of a whisper from her lips. When had she started thinking of him as Ric instead of Mr. Derby?

Just then a car drove by, breaking the trance, and he stepped back. Roberta slid into the seat again and watched as Ric started to walk behind the car to get in. If she hadn't been so focused on trying to figure out what the confused look he'd given her meant, she would have seen the car coming before it was too late.

She heard the sound of metal on metal and out of the corner of her eye, she saw Ric go flying just as she felt the jolt of the impact, as the car was hit from behind. She was out of her seat belt in seconds and besides him in less time.

he image of the black sedan, which had sped up as it turned to leave the garage, was embedded into her memory, as was the vision of Ric lying on the ground with a large gash in his shoulder and blood running down his forehead.

After she had called the police, and two of her uninformed friends had shown up to handle the scene, she'd driven Ric to the hospital herself. He'd made it clear he didn't want to ride in the ambulance and had actually wanted to drive to the hospital himself. She had finally talked him into letting her drive his car there instead. Luckily, it had only sustained minor bumper damage. The two cars next to his hadn't been so lucky.

She had sat beside him as the nurses and doctors poked at him. She'd laughed when he made funny faces after seeing the large needle one nurse wanted to shove in his forehead, so she could stitch the small gash up.

When she finally got around to giving her statement to the police, she was glad to see that her friends Bill and

Charlie were on duty. She told them her side of the story, giving every detail, down to the missing license plates on the sedan.

Less than two hours later, they were back in his car. She sat behind the wheel again, since the doctor's orders were for him not to drive for the rest of the day.

"You can just drop me off at my apartment. I'll send someone for the car later," he said, rubbing his forehead just below his new stitches.

"That's not going to happen; you're stuck with me tonight. How do you feel about watching a bunch of kids beat me up?" She smiled over at him.

"Pardon me?" He stopped massaging his head and looked at her. His shirt was slightly ripped on the shoulder and there was dried blood down his neck. His hair looked like he'd been running his hands through it and, for the first time since meeting him, he looked...well...not perfect. But she had to admit, he was sexy as hell. How had she not noticed it before? Maybe it was the suit? Maybe it was the fact that he always seemed in control. He wasn't in control now and she found that very appealing.

"Well, your little trip to the ER cost me valuable time. My class starts in less than a half hour. And your doctor gave me direct orders to watch you tonight, and I don't take orders lightly. You're stuck with me and we're going to my tae kwon do class."

His head hurt like crazy; a slight concussion was nothing to laugh at. Hearing the screaming kids did little to alleviate the pounding headache. But seeing the little kids toss the detective around was amusing. Oh, he could tell that she allowed the smaller kids to toss her about. She actually jumped around a lot and had the kids smiling with self-satisfaction. Which, of course, made him smile in return.

It actually looked like fun. He had attended self-defense classes when he was younger, but boxing had been his big thing. Sadly, it had been years since he'd strapped on the gloves. Watching her with the kids made him want to pick them up again.

Almost two hours later, they walked into his apartment. They'd stopped by her place to feed her cat, Jack, and she had grabbed an overnight bag. He'd looked around her small living room and had liked the simplicity of the space. The deep, earthy colors matched how he thought she would decorate. She was a very tidy person, and nothing was out of place. The cat had seemed to like him, rubbing around his legs until he'd heard the can opener, at which point he'd run in to eat his food.

His medicine had finally kicked in and his headache was wonderfully dull now. His shoulder still stung from the seven stitches he'd received there. The two on his forehead were just above his hairline. He wasn't a vain person, but he was thankful he wouldn't have a huge scar on it like the one he was bound to have on his shoulder.

"Would you like something to eat?" He walked towards the kitchen. His Portland apartment was not as big as the one in LA, but he still enjoyed the neighborhood, and the view of the Columbia River and Mount Hood was breathtaking. The three-bedroom apartment sat empty for a few months out of the year. Its hardwood floors and designer furniture were cleaned weekly by a maid service. The art on the walls was from his own personal collection; some of his favorite artists' pieces were hung here.

"Why don't you sit down before you fall over?" She walked him to the couch. "*I'll* make us something to eat." She pushed him back onto the couch when he just stood in front of it, looking at her.

Deciding to admit defeat, he rested his head back against the soft cushions. He listened to her moving around in his kitchen. He enjoyed cooking, so naturally, his kitchen was not only stocked, it was well stocked, and he knew she would find what she needed there.

Closing his eyes, he replayed the scene from the parking garage over and over in his mind. He was sure he had seen the bald man from the robbery behind the wheel of the sedan, but he couldn't be 100 percent sure. He hadn't even told Roberta about seeing him. He remembered seeing her face over his after hitting the ground. He must have ripped his shoulder open on something, but he couldn't remember what. He did know that the dark sedan had only just grazed his leg and hip. He knew there would be bruises all up and down his left side by tomorrow.

Roberta's face had been like a light when he'd opened his eyes in the dark garage, showing him the way to stay conscious. He'd focused on her and the pain had dissipated. She had soft eyes, soft looking lips, and he could remember what they tasted like, what they felt like.

He must have fallen asleep, because the next thing he knew, Rob was lightly shaking him awake. She was leaning over him and her hair had fallen forward. Reaching up, he ran the silky strands through his fingers. He must have been a little loopy from the drugs, but he didn't care.

Pulling her face down to his, he sampled the lips he'd been dreaming of.

She allowed him to pull her into the kiss. It took just a light tug to have her sitting across his lap. Her soft body pushed up against his and he marveled in her subtle curves. Running his hands up and down her sides, he took the kiss deeper. She must have opened a bottle of wine because he could taste its tangy sweetness on her tongue. Her hands ran over his neck and when she lightly touched his shoulder, he gasped in pain.

"Oh, I forgot. Did I hurt you?" She pulled back and looked at his shoulder.

He chuckled. "No, I'm fine." He watched her eyes focus and regretted the distraction.

She pulled back even further. "I guess we'd better eat. You need to take another pill and you're supposed to eat something first." She moved to get off his lap. He held her still for another moment.

"Rob, I think there's something here. I'd like to explore it."

"I would as well. But first and foremost, it's business. I can't be involved with someone I have an ongoing case with. It wouldn't be…"

"Kosher?" he suggested.

She laughed at him, then got off the couch, and held out her hand to help him up.

She had made spaghetti and it tasted wonderful. He passed on the wine since it would cause side effects with his medicine.

After they'd cleared the dishes, he said, "My guest room is down there." He pointed to the hallway on the left.

"My room is down here." He pointed to the opposite hall-way. "If you want to-"

"Don't even go there, Derby." He noticed the smile on her face.

"Good night." She bent and picked up her overnight bag. "I'll be waking you up every hour to check on you."

When he groaned, she said, "Doctor's orders." Then she walked down the hallway towards her room.

Pulling himself together after watching her hips sway as she walked away, he retreated into his own room. He decided a hot shower would help him relax the sore muscles that were now screaming at him.

When he'd pulled off all his clothes, he stood and looked at himself in the mirror. Already he could see nasty bruises and small cuts running up and down his whole left side. The gash in his shoulder had been stitched and bandaged.

Pulling the bandage off slowly, he looked at the clean stitch line. It was a little swollen and looked a nasty shade of red mixed with purple. The rest of him had fared okay compared to that shoulder. He must have whacked it on the cement hard. When he tried to lift his arm, he could feel the tense muscles screaming at him to stop. His head spun and he had to grab the countertop so he wouldn't pass out.

He'd take a very hot shower, maybe even use the Jacuzzi tub that sat in the overly large master bathroom. He hadn't used the huge thing once since moving in a few years ago.

Turning the handles, he got the water running so hot, the whole bathroom steamed up. It took less than fifteen minutes to fill the large tub. Hitting the buttons, he set the temperature at a hundred and the bubbles at high, then he slipped into the water and groaned as the warmth spread throughout his entire body. Why hadn't he used this thing sooner? He could feel the tension leaving him inch by inch as he laid his head back on the headrest and thought of the kiss.

Roberta set her cell phone to wake her every hour and plugged it in to make sure it would charge overnight. She looked around the guest room and thought that he'd done a good job picking the colors for the room. Had he decorated it with a particular woman in mind? Did he have many women visitors that spent their nights in the guest room instead of in his bed?

She set her overnight bag on the large queen bed. Its four-poster frame looked antique and well maintained, as did the rest of the furniture in the room. She walked into the adjoining bathroom and decided to take a quick shower. Looking down at herself, she realized she still had Ric's blood on her pants. Remembering him lying on the ground bleeding, she shivered. It had been so close.

While showering, she remembered the kiss and his warm mouth. It was a "knock your socks off" kind of kiss. She hadn't had one of those in…well…ever. At least she couldn't remember any. His mouth had been hot and the passion that had come from him had almost been blinding.

After her shower, she crawled between the satin sheets and quickly fell asleep thinking of him.

An hour later, she walked into his room to wake him and check on him. When she walked in, she was shocked to see his large bed empty. There was a soft light coming from under the bathroom door. The first thing that flashed in her mind was that he'd passed out on the bathroom floor. Rushing into the large room, she looked around and she saw him lying in the large Jacuzzi tub with its jets still on. She could see steam rising from the water. His head rested against a pillowed headrest and his eyes were closed. He looked completely relaxed and wonderfully naked.

Walking over, she took in her fill of him. The man had some great muscles, and she could see the bruises running up and down his side where he must have landed.

He was resting so that his left shoulder and arm were dangling out of the water, keeping his stitches dry. Her eyes ran down his chest and enjoyed the view of his pecs. His stomach was tight, and she could just make out a very sexy six-pack. His sandy blond hair ran in a light trail, pulling her eyes downwards. Noticing that he was hard all over, she smiled. Then her eyes moved down to his thighs, which were very muscular and covered with a light coating of blond hair. He was too tall for the bathtub, so his feet hung off the ends, resting on the ledge of the tub.

Looking back to his face, she looked at his dark eyelashes. How was it that this man was lucky enough to get very long eyelashes? She was cursed with short thin ones.

His face looked totally relaxed. Walking closer to him, she sat on the edge of the tub.

"Damn it, Ric, you should know better than to fall asleep in this thing." When he opened his eyes, she saw him focus, and then she noticed the wicked look in his eyes. She tried to pull away, but he was too quick. Before she knew it, she was crushed to his wet body. Her sleeping tee shirt and shorts were soaking wet. Her hair, which had just dried from her own shower, was wet and in her eyes now.

"I was just dreaming of you and this." His mouth was on hers again. This time, the passion was undeniable. He held her head to his with his right hand as she tried to get away. "Mmmm, you taste so good." He tried to pull her closer.

"Stop it, Ric! You're going to get your shoulder wet." She pulled back and tried to hold him at bay. When he let her go, she tried to pull herself out of the large tub and almost fell on her head. Thank goodness he'd reached over and helped to steady her.

"Now, what am I going to wear to bed?" She mumbled to herself as she looked down at her wet clothes. She stood in front of the large mirror and watched him pull himself out of the tub as he laughed at her.

"Nothing." He gave her a wicked smile. "You know, I sleep in nothing, too. Maybe we should do it together?" He walked over and grabbed a towel and, after tossing her one, started to dry himself off.

"Oh, thank you, kind sir, for that more than generous offer. But, I'll pass…tonight." She walked out of the room, slipping on the wet tile as she tried to dry herself off.

CHAPTER 9

The next morning, after dropping Rob off at her office, Ric ran a half dozen errands that he'd needed to take care of. When he walked into his gallery just after one, he was surprised to see his sister leaning against the front counter talking to Kimberly.

"Katie, what are you doing here?" he asked, as she rushed towards him. She stopped cold, halfway across the room.

"Oh my god! What happened to you?" She rushed the rest of the way to his side.

He knew what she saw. The bruising had spread throughout the night. His whole forehead looked like he'd bashed it against the wall. He was thankful she couldn't see his shoulder and hip. He'd winced at the colors he'd seen in the mirror that morning. He was stiff and sore all over.

"I had a little run-in with a car," he smiled. "The car won."

"When did this happen?" she asked as he tried to pull her towards the stairs. He nodded to Kimberly who looked very concerned as well.

"I'm fine," he assured her before pulling his sister up the stairs. "It happened last night. I was going to call you, but I had company over," he said climbing the stairs with her in tow.

"Company?" She stopped on the top stair and smiled. "Anyone, I know?" His sister was always one to hear and spread the latest gossip.

"Not that kind of company. Although, I wouldn't mind..." He saw his sister's eager face. "Never mind. It was just a friend who had to wake me every hour for the concussion."

"Oh, Ric! A concussion." She ran over to him again and grabbed his head in her hands and looked more closely at his forehead. "You have stitches too. Did you call mom or dad?"

"No, why would I?"

"Well, if they found out from someone else, they would be frantic."

"Katie, I'm a big boy. If I need them, I'll call them. Besides Dad is still in Alaska and Mom...well...I think she's..." His mind flashed to an image of Dante Cardone. "I think she's still in Italy."

"Oh, well. I'm here now. I can take care of you."

"No! Please!" he said a little too quickly. "I can care for myself. Besides, the last time you saw fit to take 'care' of me, I remember ending up in the hospital with food poisoning."

"It wasn't my fault that the chicken you had in your fridge was bad. My chicken soup was perfect. If you had bought good chicken…" she took a big breath. "Let's not rehash the past."

"Yes, let's not." He smiled at her as he sat behind his desk. "So, what brings you to Portland?"

"Well, it's spring break this week and the rest of my friends are on the beach somewhere, but I just wanted to come to visit my big brother."

"Who are you and what have you done with my sister?"

"Oh, okay! I'm worried about Mom. Do you know I called her at her hotel the other day and a man answered? A very *Italian* sounding man! Did I mention it was almost midnight there?" She got up and started pacing in front of his desk as she rambled on. "Ric, what is a very Italian man doing in Mom's hotel at midnight? I hung up immediately; I didn't know what to do. You just *have* to do something."

"Are you sure you had the right number?" He leaned back in his chair. His sister always worked herself into these little episodes. Most of the time, she would call, and he could talk her down, but this time she'd actually flown across the state to vent.

"Of course, I got the right number. It's programmed in my phone. She always stays at the same place, you know that." She leaned on his desk. "What did she say to you the last time you called her? Did she mention Dad?"

"No, when I called—" He was interrupted by his phone. Holding his finger up he motioned for his sister to sit and wait.

"Ric Derby," he answered. "Send her up, please." He

knew that his smile got huge, but he didn't care. He saw his sister's eyebrows raise, then Roberta walked into his office, and he saw that she too wore a Cheshire grin.

"Hello," Rob said. "I didn't mean to interrupt."

His sister stood and looked at the woman who had Ric grinning like a schoolboy.

"Rob, this is my sister, Katie. Katie, this is Detective Roberta Stanton. Rob is handling the case of my break-in."

"Hello, it's nice to meet you. Ric has told me so much about you. Spring break?" Rob asked.

Katie smiled and nodded her head. "Thank you for taking care of my brother last night."

Ric looked at his sister. The little brat knew too much, so he jumped in.

"Have you eaten lunch yet?" His question was aimed at Rob, but his sister piped in.

"Oh, what a wonderful idea. I'm starved. Roberta, would you care to join us? I'd love to hear all about how you became a detective." His sister reached over and took Rob's arm, then started steering her towards the stairs.

It was several hours later when Roberta let herself into her apartment. Jack came and rubbed himself all over her boots, no doubt wanting his dinner.

Instantly her senses went on alert. Something wasn't right. Pulling her service weapon out, she checked the place over. Nothing. Holstering her weapon, she stood in the middle of the room and scanned her living space. What could have caused her to be on alert? She wasn't one to freak at the smallest things. She'd been alone for most of her life and wasn't a girl who jumped at shadows. Something was out of place in her apartment. Jack seemed to think nothing was amiss, except for the lack of food in his bowl. She started to get him a can of wet food when she saw it.

Something strange sat on her kitchen counter, right next to her answering machine. Walking over, she picked up the small pin, rolling it over in her hand. She knew for a fact that she'd never seen this pin before. It looked like a quarter, and the shiny silver front had a symbol that she'd only seen once in her life. Rushing to her closet, she pulled out a box from the top shelf. It took some maneuvering, but finally, the box sprung free from its spot wedged between two boxes of old shoes. Sitting down on the edge of the bed, she opened the box that held the last memories of her father.

Digging around, she was beginning to think she'd lost it when her fingers touched the small disc. Running her thumb over her father's medallion, she held the matching pair side by side.

Someone had been in her apartment. Who had it been? What did this mean? Why had they left this here? So many other questions ran through her mind.

When Jack jumped up in her lap and rubbed his face on hers, she set the medallions down next to the box and went to feed the starving, ten-pound feline.

Rob was having one of those days she wished she'd stayed

in bed. It seemed like nothing was going right. She not only wished she had stayed in bed, she wished that everyone would just leave her alone.

Jack had tripped her when she'd gotten out of bed, and she'd ended up on the floor in a tangled pile. He had taken the opportunity to come and lay on her chest, demanding more food. Then her water heater pilot light had gone out, which of course, she hadn't noticed until after she'd gotten naked and wet. She had just tolerated the cold shower, rather than running outside to relight it.

On her drive into work, her car had acted up, as well. It had sputtered and backfired when she'd parked in the garage, which had caused several people who had been entering the building to look over and watch her exit her car.

But the icing on the cake had been when she'd walked in and seen Dante Cardone sitting at her desk. She didn't want to deal with him right now. She had the two matching medallions tucked in her pocket and she needed to do some research. Marching over to her desk, she tried to ignore a headache that was slowly building behind her eyes.

"Mr. Cardone is there something I can do for you?" She sat down and silently wished away the stacks of paper-work, which were piled so high on her desk that they were leaning.

"Hello again, Detective." She noticed that he deepened his accent when he spoke to her. "Your partner told me I could wait here for you. Yes, I would like to open a report to have this"—he tapped a folder that was sitting on her desk— "officially reported as stolen. My insurance agent informed me that I needed a police report. It appears that my…that Mr. Derby and The Blue Spot are willing to work on trying to fix this matter and it appears that this might have something to do with the theft and murder at his gallery."

"You could have filled out this report with my partner." She waited as he shifted in his seat uncomfortably.

"Yes, well. I wanted to take a chance that you were on duty." He smiled at her and she realized that he actually looked more like Katie than Ric.

"Is there any chance we could go somewhere? Lunch maybe?"

"Are you asking me to lunch for a professional reason or a personal one?" She was getting irritated now because she could see that he actually thought he was getting somewhere with her.

He shifted gears again and tried to pour on his charm by smiling smoothly and leaning closer. She continued to look at him, not taking his bait and waited it out.

She had always loved playing the game. She could usually read people. Guilty people usually didn't look you in your eyes. People who had something to hide would look, but then quickly turn away. People who had nothing to hide could stare you down most of the time. Dante Cardone had something to hide.

"Well"—he shifted uncomfortably now— "I wanted to make sure that you didn't think of me as a suspect in Mr. Derby's case."

She smiled a tight smile. "Let me assure you, Mr. Cardone, that if you were a suspect in this or any other cases, you would know when I wanted you to know and no sooner." She stood and handed him a form. "Fill this out and you can turn it in at the front desk. Now, if you will excuse me, I have other matters to see to."

Walking down the hall without looking back, she entered the geek's office. Well, that's what she called Ryan McAllen. He was a twenty-something kid who was faster on the computer than anyone she'd ever seen. He could crack any firewalls or websites, hack any email, and track all spam and viruses. And he'd always been able to make Google cough up the answers that she could never seem to find.

When she walked into the dark room, his four monitors, which were the only light source in the room, illuminated his thin face. His wire-rim glasses always seemed to be dirty. His thick dark hair stood up like he'd been running his hands through it or he'd forgotten to comb it that day.

"Hey, Mic." She knew he hated it when everyone called him that, but the nickname had stuck since day one. "I need your help with something." She flipped on the lights and could have sworn she heard him hiss. Taking a seat next to him, she pulled out the medallions she'd been carrying since discovering the one in her apartment.

"What?" he asked impatiently.

"I need to find out more about this symbol." She set the two pieces down.

He leaned over the desk and looked at them, then returned to his computer screen without a word.

It took him less than five minutes to have a matching picture with information on his screen.

"I'll print everything up for you, but from the looks of it, you're looking at two coins from Bahia, Brazil. They appear to be from the sixteen hundred. Very old, very valuable. Where did you get these?" He turned to look at her, but she just looked at him.

"You know, there's a myth about the first gold coins in Brazil." He typed in something else and another screen came up.

"Here," he pointed. "It says that gold was discovered in Brazil in the late 1600s and most coins made around then were later melted and turned into guineas. But the myth states that a handful of coins had surfaced before gold had been officially discovered in Bahia." He turned and looked at her again, this time swiveling his whole chair. He paused for effect. "You've heard of the legend of El Dorado." He tapped his desk and held back a laugh.

Roberta laughed. "You have got to be joking. Kid, you need to get out more. First off, these"—she picked up the two pieces— "aren't even gold. They are..." Looking down at them, she realized she didn't quite know what they were. "Silver? Second off, there is no way my old man would have kept anything valuable lying around in an old shoe box if he knew he could pinch it for enough liquor to last the rest of his miserable life."

"Look, I'm just relaying the myth here. Take this." He reached over and handed her the stacks of paperwork he'd printed. "Read about your coins and maybe you'll find the answers." Then he turned back around and cleared his screen and began working again. "Oh, and hit the lights on your way out," he called over his shoulder.

Rob walked out of the dark office with her stack of papers, wondering how the damn thing had ended up in her place. She didn't think her father had any living relatives. At least he'd never talked about his family. To be honest, she didn't even know her grandparents' names on either side. Then a thought crossed her mind. Quickly doing some basic math, she realized that they could still be alive.

Making her way back to her desk, she sat down to do some digging on her family history.

CHAPTER 10

atie Derby sat in her brother's apartment bored out of her mind. How could her brother stand to be on a business call for two whole hours?

She hadn't decided what to major in, much less what she was going to do after college, but whatever she did decide to do, she was going to damn well make sure it didn't involve being on the phone for two hours on a Friday night.

Flipping through the channels on his large flat-screen TV, she ended up watching the news and thinking about Jason. Jason Keaton had been on her mind for years. He was her best friend, her roommate, her confidante, the only man she'd ever wanted to be with. Ever since leaving Boston, she'd checked her phone for messages every five minutes.

If her brother knew that the real reason she was in town was to show Jason she didn't need him, she was sure he'd send her packing. She and Ric were made of stronger stuff; they had never run away from anything, including their problems. They faced them and tore down anything that got in their way. Not like their parents; for them, running to different corners of the globe had been a standard.

Checking her phone for messages again, she wasn't surprised to not see any. Not even Brenda, her best friend since second grade, had messaged her all weekend. Brenda, along with four of her other friends, had decided to spend the weekend in Mexico. Basking in the sun, picking up guys, and drinking all night didn't sound like much fun to Katie right now, but maybe the beach would have been better than here?

Looking around her brother's sparkling apartment, she wondered why she'd bothered to come here at all. She could be at the beach, getting over the kiss and the embarrassment she had caused herself with Jason. Maybe she would call and get a flight for the next day.

Just then she looked up to see her brother walking in. He really did look like someone had beat him over the head with a baseball bat. Every time she saw him, she cringed, knowing he must be in terrible pain.

Meeting Roberta—Rob as she'd told her to call her—had been the only highlight of the weekend so far. Knowing she had something to hang over her dear brother's head, she smiled and decided he could take a little more poking from his sister.

Ric hated dealing with lawyers and insurance agents. Having the art stolen from his gallery was easier to deal with than having something stolen as it was being delivered. Even though Roberta had filled out the police report, which he had multiple copies of, he still had to explain to three different agents and two different lawyers what had happened. Couldn't they just look at the damn reports?

His head was throbbing as he walked back into his living room. His sister's dark head bounced up when she heard him walk into the room. His television was on the news and was about twenty decibels louder than he would have liked.

Walking into the kitchen, he poured himself a glass of water and downed his medications.

"No, you don't," his sister said as she walked into the room. "You aren't supposed to take those on an empty stomach. Besides, you promised me you would take me out tonight."

Looking at her, you wouldn't think they were related. Where Ric was tall with sandy blond hair and blue eyes, his sister was shorter with dark wavy hair, and she had eyes the color of his old chestnut horse, Caramel. He'd actually called her Caramel Katie for most of their childhood.

Leaning against the counter he watched her check her phone for the millionth time.

"Expecting a call?" He laughed at the face she made at him.

"I think Rob is really very pretty. Don't you?" She crossed her arms over her chest mimicking him.

"Touché." He laughed with her. "Come on, I know this great little pizzeria just down the street."

Rob was ready to pull her hair out. She was spending her days hunched over case files and her nights hunched over her computer, trying to track down her father's family.

She had his police record and the large file sat on her desk next to her laptop. She knew her mother's name was Mary Catelani—at least that's what her father always told her it was—but so far, she hadn't come up with any clues as to where her family had come from. Her father had always told her that her mother had died in a car accident in Seattle when Rob was four. She'd pulled the records from the Seattle PD for any deaths involving that name within the right time frame. Nothing. She'd searched the whole state of Washington's database. Again, she'd come up empty.

Then less than five minutes ago, she'd finally found her answers. Her mother's name was Maria Catalonia, and she'd been just seventeen when she'd given birth to Rob. She'd listed the father as unknown on her birth certificate. It appeared that her mother was still alive.

A week after Rob had been born with the name of Ruth Ann Catalonia, she'd been stolen from her grandparents' house and never seen again. Her grandparents had offered a reward of ten thousand dollars for any information leading to the whereabouts of their granddaughter, whom they had full custody of at the time.

Ruth Catalonia. Her mind was spinning. She typed that name and the name of the small town in Washington that her grandparents had lived in at the time.

Old news articles came up, one with a picture of a small dark-haired baby girl dressed in a light pink floral gown.

~

Rob sat there and looked at herself as a baby. For the first time in her life, she knew that her father hadn't just stolen her childhood, he'd actually stolen her.

~

The next few days with his sister seemed to fly by. It had only taken her two days to destroy his guest room, and another day to pack her stuff and get a flight to Mexico to go be with her friends.

She apparently never received the call she'd been looking for and, on several occasions, he'd tried to talk to her about it. Every time, she would just change the subject to Roberta or their parents.

He thought of Rob more often now. She'd called a few times to update him on his case, and each time he'd enjoyed her voice and realized how much he missed seeing her.

He was sitting in his office late one night, thinking about her, when Kimberly knocked on his door. "I'm just heading out for the night. Oh, Detective Stanton is waiting for you downstairs. Shall I tell her to come on up?"

Standing, Ric replied, "No, I'm just leaving myself. I'll come down. Goodnight, Kimberly."

Shutting his door behind him, he followed Kimberly down the stairs and watched her walk out the front door. He turned and flipped the lock behind her. He'd expected to see Rob walking around in the main gallery. Instead, he found her standing next to the window in his storeroom. She looked lost and sad as she gazed out at the rainy night.

"Detective?" He saw her jump. "Is there something I can do for you?" She turned towards him, leaning against the windowsill.

"Well, it appears that Kenny Sorvillo, your bald art thief, was found this morning floating face down in the Columbia River. The weird part is that he'd been beaten, stabbed twenty-eight times, and shot five times." She turned and looked out the window again. "We still haven't found the other two men who helped him out."

"You came all this way on a rainy night to give me an update on my case?" He walked closer. He could tell there was something bothering her. He waited to see if she would open up to him.

She took a deep breath.

It had been chewing at her insides for days. She hadn't talked to anyone else about what she'd found out. How could she? She'd known her father was a bottom-feeder her whole life. But to actually steal a baby?

After more research, she'd found out that her mother had eventually married. She even had a half-brother out there somewhere, just a few years younger than she was. How many cold nights had Rob wished for someone to love her?

Her father had taken everything away from her. Yet she was torn between hate and love for the man. He hadn't been such a bad guy all the time, just when he drank. She'd never once been told to brush her teeth, go to bed early, or do her homework. He'd trusted her to know that those things should be done, and she'd done them.

Looking at it in clear light, she realized what had probably happened. They'd had an affair, Maria had gotten pregnant, and she'd told her family she didn't know who the father was. She had too many of his traits not to be part of her old man. He must have found out Maria had given up custody of her to her grandparents, and he'd snuck in and taken her as a baby. That was the only explanation she could come up with. That was how she hoped it had been.

Turning now, she looked into Ric's eyes. She saw the concern and it ate at her.

"Did you know that when I was seventeen, I broke into this building?" She patted the windowsill. "I crawled in this window, opened a safe sitting just there." She pointed to the corner. If she closed her eyes, she could still see the old black safe in her mind. "I took twelve hundred dollars in cash and this." She held up her right hand and showed him the gold ring that glimmered on her finger. She didn't realize tears were streaming down her face until he stepped closer and gently wiped them with his thumb.

"I walked back to my friends and we went to celebrate. They were all gunned down that night and it was my fault. All my fault. I've never told anyone about what really happened that night."

She took a deep breath. "Just like I haven't told anyone else what I just found out this week. My father stole me from my grandparents' house when I was a week old." She pulled away from him and hugged herself.

"He raised me by himself, knowing that they were looking for me. He taught me to be a thief, showed me how to pick pockets almost before I could walk and how to crack a safe when most ten-year-olds were tucked warmly in their beds. Then, when I was older, he'd hit me after drinking too much. Hit me until things would break, until I almost broke." Ric pulled her into a light hug.

"I'm so sorry…" he started.

"I'm not." She pulled back and looked at him. "Over the last few days, I've thought about it."

Pulling further away, she quickly dashed away the tears. "I wouldn't be where I am now if it hadn't been for that man. If it hadn't been for that night over ten years ago. And if it hadn't been for Detective Johns. I can't look back. I'm Roberta Stanton, ex-thief, detective, and I love my job, I love the people I work with, I love my apartment, my old car, and I even love my stupid cat."

Ric smiled. "You are the strongest woman I know." He walked up to her again and placed a soft kiss on her lips. "I'm not sorry you are who you are, either." Upon her empty look, he continued, "I would have never met the sexy, spitfire detective who has me thinking about her all the time."

Rob laughed. "Is that really what you think of me?"

He smiled at her, then he was kissing her and answering her question. His lips were warm and soothing. She held onto his shoulders as his tongue played with hers. She felt a shiver run down her spine when his lips set a trail down her neck. She arched back to give him better access. Running her hands over his shoulders, she enjoyed the smoothness of his suit. He was neat and prim and she really wanted to mess him up. Tugging his shirt from his pants, she ran her hands up his chest and enjoyed the feel of every muscle. She'd seen his body, all of it, and knew just how wonderful he looked.

He returned the favor and pulled her shirt free from her pants. His warm fingers sent shivers up her spine as he roamed higher and higher until finally, her hands fell away from him and she was gasping for air as he gently stroked her delicate skin.

Leaning against the brick wall, she moaned his name as he bent his head and replaced his hands with his mouth.

The wall was cool on her back as Ric's mouth claimed her skin, heating her up from her core. She grabbed his hair and held on as he tortured her, running his hands up and down her sides.

She reached for his belt and tried to pull it from his pants, but he took her hands and pulled them beside her head and looked into her eyes. They were both gasping for breath and she could see the matching desires in his eyes.

"Wait," he said and leaned his forehead against hers. "Let's just slow down a minute." He closed his eyes.

Closing her eyes, she rested her head back against the brick wall.

She wanted the sex, she wanted it with him, fast, here against the wall, in this room with so much history. Damn the consequences. Thank goodness he'd had the sense to stop.

"Listen, Ric—" she started, but he interrupted.

"Don't." He leaned back and took a deep breath. "Don't tell me this was a mistake. Because we both know it wasn't." Tucking in his shirt as she tucked in hers, he smiled at her. "How about we go get some dinner?"

She laughed. "Sure, how about we swing by Barb's. I'm in the mood for a greasy burger."

Two days later, the bruises on his face were completely

healed, but he still had tender spots on his head. His shoulder still felt stiff, but the stitches were finally gone. He'd been given the go-ahead from his doctor to start lifting weights and running again. Running had been something he'd done almost every day for the past twenty years. Giving it up for those few days had been like giving up caffeine.

The next morning as he was jogging on the riverfront pathway, he couldn't help but feel more rooted. The sun was just rising, bouncing off the river as he took his favorite path.

He could smell summer coming and knew he'd be heading to California in a few months to stay there for a few weeks. He wondered why he continued to divide his time so much. He really did enjoy Portland and the slower lifestyle here more than the fog and fast pace of downtown LA. He had several galleries across the US. Why did he keep splitting his time between these two? He knew that LA was the hot spot for a lot of the art world. New York was, as well, but he only traveled there once or twice a year.

It's not as if he was needed at any of his locations for any given time. He occasionally flew in to town for a show or a meeting, but for the most part, he could successfully run everything from this office. He'd thought about staying in Portland full time more and more over the last few years.

His thoughts turned towards Roberta. He'd never enjoyed someone's company as much as hers. When they'd eaten at Barb's the other night, they hadn't had to work at the conversation. She wasn't just damn sexy, but smart and witty. They'd laughed and enjoyed each other so much that they'd stayed at the restaurant until after eleven that night.

Every time he thought of her, he found it hard to concentrate on anything else. He'd just hit the three-mile mark in his run and was turning around to start heading back when he felt the hairs on the back of his neck stand up.

The jogging path was well traveled, and he always ended up passing a dozen or so people on his morning runs. However, as he looked around now, he couldn't see anyone else in sight. Maybe that was the reason for his alarm since he was hardly ever alone on the trail. Pulling his earbuds out of his ears, he listened and looked around. He didn't hear or see anything and had started jogging again when a sharp burning pain exploded on his side and he heard the gunshot.

CHAPTER 11

*R*oberta was just leaving the chief's office with her partner Tom, Sergeant Johns, and three other officers when she received a call on her cell phone from Ric.

"I'm being shot at—running trail twelve along the river —three miles from my apart—" She heard a round of shots and the line went dead.

Jumping up, she relayed the message as she and her partner ran through the building, heading for their car. As she ran she tried to call him, but it went to his voice mail, so she texted him in hopes that he would see it.

"Be there in two minutes. Stay down. Stay alive. Rob."

She broke every speed record she could to get there, to get to him. When she pulled the squad car up onto the dirt trail, she saw Ric sitting on a bench surrounded by a half dozen people in bright running suits.

The paramedics pulled in behind her as she sprinted from the car and ran towards him. When she got closer, she saw the blood on him and her concern tripled.

"I'm okay," he said holding up his hand as she approached. "It's just a graze. Dr. Kim, here"—he nodded to an elderly Asian man who was decked out in a bright orange running suit—"has taken a look and assured me it's just a graze. He doesn't even think I'll need stitches…this time." She could tell he was trying to calm himself down and noticed he wasn't doing a good job at it. She saw that his hands were shaking as he held his bloodied tee shirt against the wound that no doubt would just need some cleaning.

Squatting down next to him, she looked into his face; he was paler than his normal tan glow. His hands were still shaking, and she could tell he was pissed.

"Tell me what happened," she said as the paramedics started to check him out.

"Well, there I was, enjoying my first run in over a week, when, bam, someone shot at me." She knew he was trying to use humor to mask the fear. "And they didn't stop; they unloaded several rounds trying to get to me."

"I've never seen a man move so fast," Dr. Kim piped in. "If my running team hadn't been around the corner and heard it all, I think Mr. Derby here would have been a goner."

"What do you mean?" Rob asked, looking up at the man.

"Well, the shooter was reloading his gun when we came running across the bridge and I guess we must have scared him off. The man was calmly walking to where Mr. Derby was hiding behind that tree." Dr. Kim pointed to a large oak. From where Rob was kneeling, she could see the trunk had been sprayed with bullets.

"Tom, would you take Dr. Kim and his group's statements. I'll take Mr. Derby's." Rob didn't take her eyes off Ric's face.

"Sure thing, Rob. Dr. Kim, did you get a good look…" She tuned her partner's questions out.

"Are you okay?" She'd seen the large gash across his left ribs that marked where a bullet had been inches away from going straight through his side.

"I had just taken my earbuds out. If I hadn't, I wouldn't have heard and reacted so quickly." He looked down as the EMT was placing a large bandage over the open wound. "This was personal, it felt personal."

"We're all done here," the EMT interrupted. "You'll need to make sure that stays clean. Maybe take something over the counter for any pain. If you see any swelling or signs of infection, see your doctor."

As Ric stood, she watched him test himself. His face was still paler than normal. His shirt was a complete loss. Grabbing his arm, she said, "Hang on a minute." When he nodded, she walked over to her partner.

"Tom, I'm going to drive Mr. Derby back to his apartment. Can you get a ride from…" she looked around and saw two other cops from their unit and nodded towards the pair.

"Sure thing, Rob, don't worry about me. I'll write this up, help them pull evidence, and have it on your desk."

"Thanks." She walked to where Ric stood, looking down at his blood-covered hands.

A memory flashed in her mind of her looking down at her own bloody hands, and something shifted inside her.

"Come on, let's go get you cleaned up."

⚮

Sitting in Rob's car as she drove him the short distance back to his place, Ric's mind played over the scene several times.

She'd given him some wipes so he could clean up. He looked down and was glad to see his hands clean of all the blood.

When he'd been lying behind the tree, escaping the bullets, his mind had kept flashing to Roberta's face. Looking over at her now, he could see the worry in her eyes. He'd seen pure fear there when she'd sprinted towards him on the running path.

Smiling, he realized she'd been truly afraid. Did it mean that she had feelings for him? Watching her drive, he smiled, even more, realizing he had feelings for her. What kind of feelings, exactly, he didn't quite know yet, but he was willing to try and figure them out. After all, he had time.

"Keep looking at me like that and I'll start shooting at you myself." She said, stealing a quick glance at him.

He laughed, as they pulled into his parking garage.

"I'll walk you up."

He looked at her, raising his eyebrows in question.

She explained, "I need to officially take your statement."

He thought he saw her cheeks turning pink, so he just nodded.

The car ride had been bad enough, but it seemed to him that all the air had been sucked out of the elevator. The short trip up to his floor seemed to take longer than usual. He stood across the small space and just looked at her. Her eyes were glued to his bare chest and arms.

He could see her desire plainly written in her eyes, and

it most likely mirrored his. Finally, the doors slid open and she walked out slowly. He followed and watched the way she walked, the way her hips swayed in the light tan slacks that she wore today. She had on a dark blue button-up blouse, and he wondered what was underneath it all.

When he opened the door to his apartment, he watched her walk in first. When she stopped just inside the door, he pushed the door closed with his foot, not taking his eyes off her. Then she was on him, pushing his back against the cool wood of the door. Her hot mouth was on his, her hands fisted in his hair. He lost all ability to think. She was a wildcat, her lips and hands traveled all over his face and arms.

He fisted his hands on her hips and pushed her until their positions were reversed. Pulling her shirt free, he ran his hands up until he cupped her silky breast.

Releasing a low moan, she continued running kisses over his face and neck while her fingernails bit softly into his shoulders.

He ran his hands up her neck and tugged her hair free from the large clip. He enjoyed running his hands through the long, dark tresses.

She arched her neck, exposing her soft skin for him to rain kisses along her jawline. His hands were back under her shirt, playing with the soft skin underneath. He could feel her nipples straining against the silk of her bra. He wanted to taste her, wanted to take her, there against his door. Hard, fast, now.

He started to reach around and pull her upwards towards him when his hands ran into her holster, and her weapon. It was like a large bucket of ice water had just hit him square in the chest.

Pulling back, he watched her face as she realized it herself. She took a large breath and closed her eyes, then leaned her head back on the door.

"I'm sorry," she said.

"No, don't be sorry." Pulling her face into his hands, he held her until she opened her eyes and looked at him.

"We will finish this." He didn't know if he was promising her or warning her.

She looked at him and just nodded her head. He stepped back and watched her tuck her shirt back into her belt.

"Did your sister leave?" She looked around.

"Yeah." He picked up his ruined shirt and tossed it in the trash. "She headed to Mexico to be with her friends." He watched her walk around the large room and thought she might be trying to get under control. Her arms were crossed over her chest and she was pacing his living area. She looked like she was stalling.

"What do you want, Detective?"

She spun around quickly and looked at him.

"What do you want to drink?" He held up a bottle of water and noticed that something flashed in her eyes.

"No, nothing. I'm fine." She continued pacing the room.

Taking a large swig of water, he walked over to stop her nervous walking by grabbing onto her shoulders. Looking into her eyes, he saw her raw emotions.

Pulling her close, he held on tight as she went into his arms.

"Thank you," he said.

"Why are you thanking me?" She leaned back and

looked up into his eyes. He took advantage and leaned down to claim her mouth softly.

"Thank you for being there for me."

"I should have gotten there faster. It wasn't me that saved you; it was Dr. Kim and his running group."

"You were there. When I was hiding behind that tree, all I could think of was you." He looked into her eyes and saw shock.

"I don't know what to do with this information. Do you expect me to—?"

"Shh, I don't expect anything. Just know that I thought of you."

He pulled her into another light hug.

"You know, since I met you, I seem to always end up bloody and bruised."

She laughed, and he enjoyed the sweet sound and vowed to hear it again and as often as possible.

"Are you going to take my"—he cleared his throat—"statement?" She smiled up at him.

What a waste of time! And even more of a waste of money. He was just glad he hadn't actually paid the man yet. He had sat in his car across from the jogging trail and watched for himself. The man he'd hired couldn't shoot a large stationary target on the side of a barn, let alone an unarmed man jogging alone. And he was sure that his hired hand had been seen by no less than half a dozen people. Something had to be done.

He knew that some pawns had to be sacrificed in order to get to the queen. Looking across the table at the skinny man who looked a little too self-confident, he thought of how he would accomplish the task. Maybe there was a way to play this where he would get what he wanted and get rid of his employee at the same time.

Smiling, he leaned back in his chair and told the man exactly what he wanted him to do.

It had taken Roberta two days to identify the shooter. Dr. Kim and his running group had been invaluable to the search. When Tom had shown everyone the lineup, each had pointed to his picture. Identifying the perp had been easy, but finding the man was a different matter.

Ricky Scoles had been in and out of jail for the past fifteen years. His rap sheet was long and went back years. When he was a juvenile, he'd been tried as an adult for a botched robbery in which two store clerks had been gunned down. He'd gotten off easy since he'd only been the driver that night. Word on the street was he was a hired hand now, taking odd jobs, working for a few of the local gangs, drug lords, even some of the hookers that still worked the East Side. The low-life scum-bucket had been a quick hire for someone. The question now was, who had hired him to kill Ric and why?

"I'm clocking out, Tom." She threw the last of her paperwork on her desk and decided the rest could wait until the morning.

She had her class later that night but figured maybe a quick stop by Ric's couldn't hurt. She texted him as she walked out to the parking garage. She knew he would be leaving the gallery soon. She had a couple of black and whites driving by his place every hour to make sure everything was going smoothly. Not to mention she'd made him promise to text every hour. He'd talked her into every other hour.

"Wanna grab some grub?" She waited for his reply.

"Sure, meet you at Barb's in twenty?"

"I'll be there."

She pushed her phone into her back pocket and reached for her keys. The first blow came out of nowhere. Her ears were ringing as she was grabbed and spun around. She got a quick glimpse of him. Tall, about one-seventy, jet-black hair—Ricky Scoles. Then she was being thrown against her car, and one of his hands went over her mouth. The other was reaching frantically for her hands.

"You're coming with me bitch. My boss wants you." His voice was husky and laced with anger.

He was trying to trap her hands in his, but she fought back, pushing his hands away. She could smell his sweat and fear.

She'd trained for this her whole life. Her instincts kicked in and it took her only a second to react. When he pulled his arm back to take another swing at her, she pushed, ducked, and kicked out, catching him off guard.

Her vision was fading from the blow to the side of her head and she was worried she might black out. Quickly dodging his next blow, she saw him reach behind to where he would keep a gun.

By the time his hands returned with the weapon, her shots rang out in the empty parking garage.

CHAPTER 12

*R*ic answered his phone after seeing his sister's number on the display.

"Have you called Mom yet?"

"Well, hello, Katie. It's nice to talk to you too," he replied.

"Yes, yes, hello. Have you *talked* to Mom yet?"

"No, I haven't *talked* to Mom yet," he mimicked.

"Ric, you told me you were going to call her days ago. I'm dying to find out who…" He heard a knock on his door and knew it was Rob. She'd called earlier and canceled their dinner plans, then told him she'd meet him at his place in a few hours.

"Hang on, Katie. Roberta's at the door."

"Ooh, don't let me keep you. I'll talk to you tomorrow. Have fun, be safe. *Call* Mom." His sister hung up quickly as he answered the door.

Rob stood leaning against his door frame and looking off towards the elevators.

"Before you freak out," she said, not looking in his

direction, "you should see the other guy." She turned, and he saw what she'd been hiding from him. The right side of her face was covered in a nasty bruise, she had a black eye, and her face was swollen. He saw a slight cut just under her right eye.

"Oh my god!" He pulled her in the door and grabbed her shoulders lightly. Looking down into her face, he could see the pain there. Her right eye was bloodshot and she winced when the bright lights in his apartment hit her full force.

"What happened?" He brushed her hair away from her temple to get a better look at the side of her face. He felt like ripping apart whoever had done this.

"Let me just apologize to you first."

"You don't have to apologize for missing dinner," he broke in.

"No, not that." She looked into his eyes. "I'm sorry that I didn't treat you with more care when you had your concussion." She smiled weakly at him and he could see the pain that the smile had caused her.

"Hmmm, you'll need someone to watch over you tonight then." He smiled slightly. "You might even want to take another Jacuzzi bath since the last time you didn't stay in it very long." He was happy when he saw a little sparkle in her eyes.

She could definitely get used to this. She'd locked herself in Ric's large bathroom. The Jacuzzi jets were set too high and the heat, along with the bubbles, was doing wonders for her bruised back and concussed head.

Ric had given up his bedroom for the night and, more importantly, he'd drawn her bath himself. He had even put a dab of scented oils in the water to help relax her, then he'd dimmed the bathroom lights as he walked out. Everything was helping with the throbbing headache she was experiencing. She'd been knocked around in the academy and by her father, but she hadn't experienced anything like this before.

She relaxed back into the hot water and thought of Ric. Then she smiled remembering when she had seen him naked in this very tub. What a body he had.

Her smaller frame easily fit in the oversized bath. When she tried to rest her head on the cushions, her feet would float up and almost suck her head under the water. She sat with her feet wedged against the bottom and her head floating in the water, which helped dull her mind.

She started thinking about her day. She had called the dojo and canceled her tae kwon do classes for the night. Actually, thanks to the doctor's orders, she had to cancel them for the next few days. And thanks to her boss, she now had those two weeks off, since he'd placed her on administrative leave, which was standard when an officer was involved in a shooting death.

Ricky Scoles was no longer going to answer any questions about who had hired him to kill Ric.

She was totally relaxed when she heard a noise. Knowing it was him, she decided to keep her eyes shut. She felt heat spread throughout her already warm body and knew he was standing there, much like she'd done last week, looking over her body.

Because of the way she'd been raised, she'd never truly experienced shame or embarrassment about her body.

She knew she was small framed with rounded curves where needed. Her arms and legs were a little on the thin side, but her muscles were toned, which made up for a lot of what she deemed to be her inadequacies.

"Well, you can see for yourself that I'm okay," she said without opening her eyes. Feeling his eyes on her did something to her insides.

"You know, I've been told one shouldn't fall asleep in that thing." His voice was getting closer to her and she could tell he stood directly over her now.

"I locked that door for a reason, Derby." She finally opened her eyes. The heat she felt didn't even compare to the fires she could see burning in his eyes.

"That's the great thing about owning a place." He held up a key ring. "You get all the keys to the doors." His smile was intoxicating and contagious.

"Well, if you're just going to stand there"—she leaned forward and tossed a washcloth to him— "you might as well work for the show you're getting."

"How about I strip down and climb in there with you?" She laughed. He walked over and leaned on the edge of the tub then started running the cloth slowly over her shoulders. "There's definitely enough room in there for the both of us."

She stretched under his fingers. "I've got a headache." She smiled into her knees, which she'd pulled up to her chest as she heard him laugh.

"No doubt." He put his finger gently under her chin and forced her to look into his blue eyes. Had she noticed how blue they were before? Or that he had a light dusting of freckles that ran across his nose? His mouth looked soft and she knew that it felt good running over her skin and against her own mouth.

"I know by the dull look in your eyes that you don't feel up to it now, but later I want all the details of what happened to you." He sobered.

She closed her eyes. Her head was still throbbing, and the medicine had done little to relieve the tension that was still building down her back. When she'd stripped naked in his bathroom and looked at herself, she'd been shocked at the colors that ran down her right side. Then she'd remembered being tossed against her car and realized why her muscles were screaming at her.

"It was stupid of me to let my guard down. I would have never done that…" she trailed off, remembering her childhood. A quick memory of her father's face came into mind. There had been plenty of times she'd ended up with worse than the bruises she had now. Broken fingers, arms, and ribs had been the norm when she was younger. Once, she even though she had a broken collarbone. She'd spent three weeks lying in bed with her father leaning over her apologizing every day. He'd quit drinking for two whole months after that incident.

"I'll be fine." She looked into his eyes. "I'm just pissed that I didn't get a chance to get some answers."

"Why don't you come out of there? I've made some hot soup and some grilled cheese sandwiches. It's almost time for you to take your medicine again." He held up a towel for her to walk into.

He waited in the living room as Roberta changed into his sweat shorts and an extra tee shirt he had laid out for her.

He had seen the pain in her eyes and knew what she was going through. While she was in the tub, he had made some calls. Sergeant Johns had filled him in on what had happened and informed Ric that Roberta was on admin leave for the next couple of weeks. He assured Ric this was only procedure. He even guaranteed that the shooting had already been deemed justified after the video from the garage had been presented.

Then he had updated him on his case, though there really wasn't an update since the two main suspects were now dead. The fact that Ricky Scoles hadn't been one of the three men to break into his galleries still weighed heavily on the investigation. They still had two other guys out there that could shed some light on the matter.

Ric had been scouring the internet since the break-in. He didn't know if these men were dumb enough to try to sell the paintings right away, but he and his staff were keeping a close eye on all the auction sites.

His mind switched to Dante's missing artwork. He didn't know what the catch was with that piece. Why had Mark taken the time and effort to steal that one himself when he'd just arranged to open the doors at his gallery that night? Why hadn't Mark just taken everything himself? Did he honestly think he wasn't going to get away? Was he planning on disappearing after everything was taken?

Since the shooting, he'd been forced into hiding by

Roberta and the police. They didn't want to take any chances with him and had asked that he not go out unnecessarily. He had his groceries delivered and was beginning to feel trapped in the apartment alone. His body had healed since his parking garage incident and since being shot at on the trails, but he'd been forced to use the treadmill in his spare room, something he tried to only use during winter.

Looking up, he watched as Roberta walked in. His sweat shorts were too big and the shirt hit her midthigh. The bruises on her face gave her a tough-girl look that he found oddly appealing. Her wet hair hung down her back in waves and he couldn't remember her looking better.

"What?" she asked him.

He had to shake his head when he realized he'd been staring at her.

"I like this look on you." He smiled.

She sat down at the table and looked at him. "You know, I thought I had you figured out."

He looked at her, waiting. She picked up the spoon and took a sip of the tomato soup and closed her eyes with pleasure. He wanted to see that look on her face for other reasons.

"I've seen photos of you, with the kind of women you find attractive, and none of them look like me. So the question is"—she took a bite of the grilled cheese— "why all the games with me?"

Looking into her eyes, he realized she was being serious. Standing up, he walked around the table and pulled her up into his arms.

"Maybe I should make myself perfectly clear." He leaned down and claimed her mouth in a slow passionate kiss. He knew he had to be gentle; just holding her face in his hands, he could see the pain there. As gently as he could, he ran his lips over hers and when she released her breath on a sigh, he dipped his tongue in for a taste and pulled her closer to him. Her hands came up and fisted in his hair, holding him to her. Running his hands down her sides, he enjoyed the contour of her hips and relished in the softness he found.

"I've never desired someone as much as I desire you right now." He looked into her eyes and then rested his forehead on hers lightly.

"Sit and eat, so you can take your pills. I can see the pain you're in. I don't like knowing you hurt."

When he sat down again, he watched her eat the rest of the sandwich and soup. Then he hustled her off to his bed and checked on her every hour. Each time, it almost killed him seeing her hair spread across his pillows. He wanted nothing more than to crawl into the big bed with her, but he kept his distance and played doctor for the night.

He stayed up late and ran several searches on his computer, trying to track down the missing art and looking for what set the Indian piece apart from the others. Around two in the morning, he finally gave up and tried to get some sleep in his guest room. He set his alarm to wake him each hour, knowing it was going to be next to impossible to get any sleep.

CHAPTER 13

*T*he next day was a little blurry for Rob. Ric had persuaded her to stay at his place for the day. He'd called in and taken the day off himself. She'd spent most of the morning asleep and woke up just before noon. When she walked into his living room, he was sitting at the dining room table with a cup of coffee, staring at his laptop screen.

"Good morning." She walked over and sat across from him. Her head still ached, and her vision was totally messed up in her right eye.

"Morning. Your partner called and wanted me relay to that he fed Jack this morning." She almost laughed at the face he was making.

"I bet that was an awkward call." When he just shrugged his shoulders, she leaned back in the chair.

"Would you like something to eat?"

"I don't expect you to wait on me. I can take care of—"

"Rob," he interrupted. "It's really not that big of a deal. I was about to fix myself a sandwich for lunch."

Smiling and feeling a little embarrassed, she nodded her head.

After lunch, he forced another pain pill on her and tucked her back into bed where she remained until the whole scene was repeated around dinnertime. This time, he ordered Chinese from the corner restaurant.

After dinner, she'd taken another bath and had propped herself up in his bed to watch the evening news, but she must have fallen asleep. When she woke again, it was the next morning, and she was feeling almost like her old self. How had he recovered in only one day?

Ric couldn't concentrate the next day. He had hardly gotten any sleep the last couple nights, which made it hard for him to focus.

His early morning meeting with clients had gone smoothly. Now he sat behind his laptop trying to deal with a few other items. He'd been doing some more research on Dante Cardone and he didn't like what he'd found.

He knew he had to make the call, but he preferred to talk to his mother in person. Calling her was always an *event*. He'd promised Katie he'd get to the bottom of the mysterious man in their mother's room. He just didn't want to hear what he thought he was going to hear from her. He stood in his office and just as he was about to pick up his phone, Rob walked in. The bruises were even more colorful today. He knew she was on admin leave, so when he saw her partner trailing behind her, he frowned. He hadn't spoken to the man often and had forgotten his name.

"Mr. Derby." She nodded her head and sat in his chair. He could see she was all business today. "You remember my partner, Detective Thomas." The tall man nodded and stood to lean against the door frame. Ric thought he looked like a guard dog watching over his pup. So this was how she was going to play him today. Smiling, he walked over and leaned on the front of his desk. "He's taking lead on your case while I'm on leave."

"What can I do for you today?" He crossed his ankles and arms.

"I've finally"—her partner cleared his throat— "*We've* finally received word from Mr. Cardone's secretary that Mr. Walker had been an employee less than a year ago at his company. He was actually still on the roster as a consultant. Did you know this when you hired him?" She looked at him.

Leaning over, he pulled Mark's file from the top of his desk. "You can see for yourself. Every reference he gave me is there. I checked them all myself. He never mentioned he worked at New Edges."

She looked over the paperwork. "Can I"—her partner coughed— "*we* keep these?"

He nodded his head. She handed the file over to her partner and started to get up.

"I'd like a moment with you, alone," Ric said, looking towards the doorway, where her watch guard was still standing, almost looking bored.

"Tom, I'll meet you downstairs in a few."

When her partner left, Ric asked, "His name is Tom Thomas?"

"Yes," she said without any hint of humor. "What did you need to talk to me about?" She crossed her legs.

His face sobered. "You were right. I'm amazed I didn't see it myself. I was just about to call my mother to have her confirm what I think I've just found out myself." He was pacing up and down in front of his desk.

"You've lost me." She uncrossed her legs and leaned forward.

"He's my brother...well, half-brother. At least I think he is..." Ric sat in the chair next to hers, looking as if he'd been kicked.

Rob came and knelt in front of him.

"You think that Dante Cardone is your half-brother?"

"Yes." He ran his hands through his hair.

"Do you want me to wait around while you make the call?"

He looked at her where she had knelt down in front of him. Her dark brown pants rested against his knees, and her hands were holding his. He unconsciously played with the gold ring on her finger.

"I don't quite know how to ask her."

"Sometimes these things need to be done in person. Where is she now?"

"Last time I heard, she was in Italy, where Dante's father runs the New Edges corporate office in Rome."

"I'll wait around if you want me to."

He stood and pulled her into a light hug. "Thank you, no. I'll call her myself. I've missed you today." He enjoyed the spicy smell of her, the soft feel of the skin just under her ear, where he touched her.

She relaxed into the hug. "How's the shoulder?"

"Fine. I'm fine. How's the head?" He smiled as he reached up and pulled her hair off of her forehead and looked at it. Then he kissed the bump there softly.

"I told myself I wasn't going to do this," she said against his chest. "What is it that keeps pulling me back to you?"

"You mean besides murder, millions of dollars' worth of missing art, me being shot at, and you being attacked?" He smiled down at her.

She chuckled. "Yes, well there is that." She tried to pull away.

"Not just yet." He leaned down and took her face in his hands and kissed her slowly. "That might get me through the rest of the day." He let her go and when she just stood there, he said, "Have dinner with me tonight."

"I can't. I have…" She was thinking.

"No good excuse?" he said as she laughed.

"Fine. Your place around six?" When he nodded she said, "Good luck with your mother."

After she walked out, he reached over and picked up the phone. On the third ring, he heard his mother's voice.

"Mom, do you have a son named Dante Cardone?" He thought the best way to handle her was to rip the Band-Aid off quickly.

"Well." She sounded like she was at a restaurant. He could hear the clatter and chatter in the background. "That's a fine way to greet me."

"Hello, Mother. Now answer my question." He waited as he heard her excuse herself and then walk someplace more private. When there was silence on the other end, she answered, "Yes." Her voice sounded small.

"Why didn't you tell us?" His heart sank.

"It was so long ago. You were so young. It was when your father and I split up that year when you were five. I met Damiano Cardone the week after I arrived in Italy to recover from the pain your father caused me. I was so heartbroken and Damiano is quite charming." Her slip caused him some alarm and he could hear her babbling on.

"*Is* quite charming, Mother?"

"Oh, Ric! I don't know what to say to you."

"Are you leaving Dad for this man?"

"No! Of course not! I didn't leave your father twenty-five years ago, why would I leave him now."

"Mother? You know what I'm asking."

"Rodrick. This is really none of your business. It has nothing to do with you."

His mother's use of his full name wasn't going to deter him from getting the answers he needed. "It has everything to do with me!" He was almost shouting at this point. "I've been doing business with this man for a few years. Does he know?"

"Dante knows who I am and that I have other children, yes. Does he know that I'm married? I don't know. But he's a smart boy."

"Did you know he's in Portland?"

"Yes, of course. His father opened the branch there a few years back when…" She cut off.

"When I opened my gallery here?"

"I don't know what you're talking about." She tried to evade him.

"Mother, I want the whole story now or I'm getting on the next plane to Italy, and I will shake it out of you."

He heard her take a large breath. "Fine. I've been leading a double life, alright! I'm married to your father, that's true. But I'm also married to Dante's father, Damiano. Our marriage, I suppose, isn't legal in the States. We were married in Italy shortly after I found out I was pregnant with Dante. When I came back to divorce your father, we ended up making up instead and I've led a double life ever since. I've been coming here to Damiano and Dante once a year for the last twenty-six years."

He could hear her pacing and knew she had talked herself into telling him everything.

"I helped raise my son until he went away to college a few years back. I also helped him start the branch of New Edges there in Portland. When I visited you a few months ago, I visited him as well. He knows about you and that is why he uses your gallery exclusively to purchase art for his clients. He's dreamed of the day he could tell you who he is. Oh, Ric!" She sounded relieved and excited. "You'll absolutely love him. He's such a good person. He'll be so happy that you've finally found out."

His head was swimming, and he sat down in his chair and put it in his hand.

"Do Katie and Dad know?" This question was met with silence. "Mother?"

"No." It was a whisper over the line.

He didn't want to ask the next obvious question because he knew the answer could break his heart.

"Does Katie belong to Dad?"

More silence. "Ric, please, I can't do this now. I...I have to go. Please don't tell your father or Katie. I'm coming home. I…I'll take the next flight. Please don't say anything until I get there."

When the line went dead, he laid his head on the cool wood of his desk and for the first time since he was a young child, he felt like crying.

There was only one way to get what you wanted. You either got it yourself, or you hired competent people to get it for you. So far, he wasn't having any luck finding someone who could do the job right. If this kept up, he was going to have to take care of Ric himself.

He'd waited long enough, longer now than he'd had to wait for anything in his entire life. After all, bloodlines were very important to him. He had a job to do, and he'd make sure he completed his task soon. Even if he had to accomplish it himself.

The little side project of getting his hands on the pretty detective was just the added bonus he was looking for. After all, it had been years since he'd had his hands on a woman he wanted. The last time was before he'd come to America. He'd be damned if he was going to wait much longer.

Rob had managed to bum around with Tom for the first part of the day. No one in the office would dare rat her out to her superiors. She knew which buttons to push or punch and whom to avoid. But she'd had to sneak out of the building just before noon when she had seen Brian coming into the office. Brian was her least favorite person on the force because he couldn't keep his mouth shut. If you wanted to know the latest gossip, Brian was usually spouting it off to someone.

Leaving the building, she was more cautious this time. She figured she had a few hours left before she was supposed to be at Ric's and might as well do a little shopping. She hated shopping. She wasn't the kind of shopper that went into a store and could walk around for hours and not buy anything. No, when she walked into a store, she usually walked out broke.

She supposed it was a side effect of having nothing when she was younger. She'd even had to start limiting her shopping sprees to one credit card so she didn't spend too much. She wasn't the kind of person who bought anything and everything. Her one weakness was boots. Boots of any kind and color. She had over a dozen pairs of them and in the last three years had spent more than…well, she didn't know exactly how much, but she had maxed out her credit cards twice, so far.

She'd forgotten to eat lunch again and by the time she entered the mall, her head was throbbing. She knew that she needed to eat something before taking her pills, so she steered herself towards the food court and her favorite Chinese noodle place.

Two hours and one pair of boots later, she made her way back to the caramel apple store she frequented.

This was one more of her weakness, caramel. Most people loved chocolate, but Roberta Stanton was no chocoholic. She was a carameloholic if there was such a word.

She was standing at the counter when the hair on the back

of her neck stood up. She positioned herself so that she could see out the front windows by looking in a small mirror that sat behind the counter, and she saw one of the men who'd been in on the robbery standing just outside the glass watching her.

Acting like nothing was wrong, she walked over to the clerk behind the counter and pointed to a display of apples.

Taking out her cell phone, she speed-dialed the office. Tom answered on the first ring.

"Hey, Tom, I'm down here at Washington Square Mall getting a caramel apple. I was going to stop and get you some shoes and was wondering what size you wore." She used their code, knowing he would immediately get her signal for backup.

"Be there in five. Are you secure?"

"Oh, yeah. Size eleven. Thanks. See you in a bit." She punched a button on her phone and slipped it into her back pocket, still connected to the line. She knew that he would trace her call and most likely have the geek squad record anything that might happen. When she exited the store, she kept her eyes on her apple and pretended not to see the man standing just behind a large potted plant. Taking her time, she walked slowly, swinging her bag with her new boots inside. She'd taken a few bites of her apple when he approached her from behind.

"Keep walking, Ms. Stanton." She felt the gun at her back and faked a gasp. "Just do as I say, and you won't get hurt. No one needs to get hurt." He pulled her arm tight and pushed her closer to him. He was a lot taller than she was and he had about eighty pounds on her, as well. She gauged her chances and decided to wait for backup; she didn't need another bump on the head.

"What do you want?" She tried to add stress and fear to her voice.

"My employer would just like a word with you. Nothing more. Just a word."

"Your employer? Who's your employer?"

"Just follow my directions and no one needs to get hurt." He started pulling her towards an employee exit that she knew led to the parking garage.

"This exit is for employees only and leads to the parking garage."

"Just be quiet." He pushed her down the long, dark hallway.

"What is this all about? You're Robbie Bender, aren't you?"

"I said shut up." He pulled her arm farther behind her and she dropped her caramel apple. They entered the parking garage, and he pushed her towards a dark sedan with tinted windows. She thought how nice it would be to catch him and his employer, all while she was on admin leave.

They approached the car slowly and just then, Tom's squad car and two others rushed into the parking garage. Robbie Bender pointed his gun at Rob's partner as he was exiting his car.

Rob performed a self-defense move she'd only practiced a handful of times. By the time her partner got to her, she had Robbie Bender on the ground. Her eyes had teared up and she was feeling as if she'd just given herself another concussion, but it had worked.

Her partner helped her up.

"That's for pointing a damn gun at my partner, scumbag." She watched as the man was yanked on to his stomach and handcuffed by another officer.

The other officers had stormed the dark sedan only to discover it was empty. A cell phone sat on one of the leather seats. Rob picked it up and listened.

She could hear breathing, then a deep accented voice said, "I had hoped you would cooperate, Ms. Stanton. But it seems you don't want to play the game fair and square. Your choice." There was a long pause. "Oh, I'll say goodbye to Mr. Derby for you." Then the line went dead.

"Shit." She threw the phone back in the seat. "He's got, Ric. Send units to his apartment and the gallery. I'm taking this car." She got in the squad car that was blocking the exit and punched the gas.

Taking her cell phone out of her pocket, she dialed Ric's cell number. It rang three times and then went to his voice mail just as she saw a large plume of smoke and a fireball coming from his apartment building three blocks away. The tall building's windows had blown out completely on his floor, and she could see smoke billowing from what she knew would be his apartment.

"Shit, shit, shit!" she screamed as she dodged a truck and narrowly avoided hitting a couple of pedestrians who hadn't heard or seen her sirens and lights. Her hands gripped the wheel as she took a corner at thirty miles an hour. Please, god, please.

She hit redial on her phone, praying for the first time in her life.

CHAPTER 14

*R*ic had left work early to prepare for Roberta's arrival. He'd made a run to the market to get fresh salmon and other items he would need to cook dinner. He was looking forward to a quiet night with her and had big plans for them tonight. Neither of them was suffering from concussions, and he wanted nothing more than to get her in his bed, this time with him in it. He'd just opened the door to his apartment when his phone rang.

Before he could answer it, he smelled something funny and knew immediately what it was. Then he heard a click. Not wasting a second, he ran towards the stairs just as everything exploded.

His ears were ringing and looking down at his hands, he realized it was his phone—which was sitting next to him on the ground—that was making the sound. Picking it up off the floor of the stairwell, he answered it.

Nothing. Ric shook his head. Either his phone was dead or he'd lost his hearing momentarily. Moving his phone to the other ear, he finally heard her screaming, "Where are you?"

"I'm in the stairs at my apartment. The place just blew up." He coughed a few times, taking stock of his body. "I'm okay. I'll come down the stairs." The smoke was quickly filling the stairway. He looked up and noticed the door had been jammed open by a large chunk of cement that had fallen from the floor above his. Then he realized he'd been tossed down half the flight of stairs. Standing up, he made sure his legs were steady. Nothing seemed to be broken or bleeding, so he took the stairs two at a time and didn't stop until he hit the ground floor. Roberta was waiting for him when he got there.

Four hours later, Ric watched Rob as she paced in front of the two-way mirror. On the other side was Robbie Bender. The man looked paler than before; if she had to guess, she'd say he was scared.

Tom was questioning him on the other side of the glass. The sergeant and the commander sat next to Ric. He'd been checked out, and they had determined that he didn't even have a scratch on him from the whole ordeal. Two of his neighbors hadn't been so lucky. One was still in surgery and the other was at the morgue.

Roberta wasn't going anywhere until she had some answers, and she wasn't letting Ric out of her sight until they had them.

"I told you, I didn't know they were going to kill that man." Robbie pointed to a picture of Mark Walker on the desk. "I don't know anything about killing him, neither."

He nodded to a picture of Kenny Sorvillo. "Last time I saw him, he was with José."

"José?" Tom leaned on the desk.

"José. You know, José. I don't know his last name. José is the one that got me this job."

Tom set down a picture taken from the gallery's surveillance cameras. "Is this José?" He pointed to the large Mexican man.

"Yeah, José got me this job," he repeated.

"Who is your boss?"

"Shit, I don't know. Only Kenny and José knew. I was just supposed to help load some shit into a truck. Then yesterday, José called me and told me to grab the pretty detective and bring her out to meet the boss.

He tried to wipe sweat from his forehead, but the handcuffs that were attached to the desk prevented him.

"Shit, I swear. I didn't know Kenny was going to whack that guy." Roberta could see the wheels working in his beady little eyes. "Hey, if you've got these"—he pointed to the photos from the tapes— "then you know I had nothing to do with shooting that guy. I mean, I freaked out when Kenny pulled that gun and shot the man."

Roberta knew it was true. Robbie had indeed freaked. Actually, she'd noted in her files that he had complained so much that Kenny had pulled the gun on him, and he'd completed the task under duress. It didn't account for the fact that less than five hours earlier, the man had shoved a loaded gun in her back.

Another hour later, she and Ric sat in the commander's office. She had an empty cup of burnt coffee and a stale doughnut in her stomach. Ric had just sat quietly drinking a bottled water, not really saying anything during this whole process. After the interrogation was over, he'd stepped into the hallway and made a few calls, she assumed to his parents or sister.

Tom had stopped by Rob's place and checked up on Jack. Her apartment had been untouched. He'd taken Jack to his place and assured her that Tammy, his wife, was happy to watch him until things settled down. She didn't need the extra stress of worrying about her baby during this mess.

Tom had packed her a bag and had tried to convince her to stay at his place. The truth was, she didn't know where she was going to go, but wherever she went, she was sure Ric was going with her.

"That settles it." Her commander, Wallas Steinkeller, was the only person that she hadn't gotten to know personally in her ten years on the force. He liked to keep his personal life quiet, but she knew that he had two daughters. Their identical smiles showed in the many pictures displayed around his office. Rob didn't know if he was married or not.

"Settles what, sir?" She leaned forward and stifled a yawn. It was almost midnight and the office was on night mode. The nights were sometimes busier than the days, but tonight wasn't one of those nights.

"You and Mr. Derby are going underground for a few weeks."

"What?" She jumped out of her chair. "You can't do this to me. I'm lead in—"

"You were lead," the commander broke in. "It says here you're on admin leave for two weeks. Sit down, Detective." She sat again, feeling defeated.

"Do you have someplace in mind for us to go?" Ric

asked calmly. How could the man be so calm? His apartment had just blown up. Everything he owned was gone. Damn, she was going to miss that Jacuzzi tub.

"Not yet, but I can pull some strings…"

"May I make a suggestion?" When the commander nodded, he continued. "I have some friends—it's not a well-known connection. No one would trace us there. It's close enough we could be back in the city in just over two hours. It's quiet and the locals would notice anyone strange in town. Plus, I've already made arrangements."

She looked over at him and was shocked to see a smile on his face.

A few hours later, just as the sun was starting to make its appearance in the east, Roberta sat back in the car and watched Ric drive the country roads with ease. Didn't he need sleep? She was working on four cups of coffee, two diet cokes, and a Snickers bar. The sugar rush had helped her finish the long meeting, but now the sugar high had dissipated, and she had started to doze off several times during the long drive.

She'd never been this far south before. She and her father had spent their whole lives in Portland and, with the exception of her quick journey overseas, she'd never really been anywhere else. For most of the trip, it had been too dark to see anything, but now with the sunlight brightening up the sky, she could just make out the shapes of trees, barns, and open fields.

They hadn't talked much during the drive. The bag that her partner Tom had packed for her was sitting in the back seat along with a small suitcase belonging to Ric, which he said had been packed and left in the trunk of his car for emergency trips.

They were supposed to stay out of touch for two whole weeks. No calls and no contact with the main office, except for emergencies. She'd never been away from her family for that long. She'd been given back her service weapon, but under the dire circumstances, the commander had revoked her admin leave and placed her on protective services instead.

Her main focus for the next weeks was keeping herself and Ric Derby alive while her friends found out who Robbie Bender and José's boss was.

She must have dozed off for a while. When the car stopped, she jumped.

"Easy," Ric said, smiling at her. "We're here." He nodded to a large white house.

"We're staying here?" She was shocked. The place was huge. The large two-story house had long green shutters on either side of the picture windows that lined the front of the place. A huge covered porch ran the entire length of the house and there were wicker rocking chairs and a swing on the porch.

"No, this is Megan and Todd's place." He smiled as he got out, then walked around the car to open her door. "We're staying in the honeymoon cabin."

She looked at him and his smile got bigger. Just then, a tall, very pregnant blonde woman walked out of the front door holding a little girl.

"Ric," the woman said as he walked up the steps. "It's so good to see you again." She walked into his waiting arms. Roberta could feel the raw emotions from both of them as they hugged. He placed a light kiss on her cheek.

"Me too." The little girl puckered her lips and Ric

kissed them and took the girl from the woman and spun her in circles.

"How is my Sara bug?" He kissed her chubby cheeks, causing the little girl to squeal with delight.

"I'm three." She held up four little chubby fingers and smiled. Roberta's heart did a little spin. She was, by far, the cutest little girl she'd ever seen.

Ric just laughed and kissed her again. "Megan, this is Roberta. Rob, this is Megan Jordan and her daughter, Sara." He looked around. "Where is my little buddy Matthew?"

"He's at school, first grade. Can you believe it?" Megan sat down on a chair and patted the seat next to her for Rob to sit.

Rob had only been this close to a pregnant woman once before, in an elevator. She'd worried the entire time that the elevator would break down and the woman would go into labor, like in the scenes she'd seen in so many movies.

"I'm not due until later next month," Megan said, laughing. Feeling a little uncomfortable, Rob sat next to the woman.

Ric sat in the swing with Sara and kicked off, causing the little girl to squeal in delight.

He looked good with a kid next to him. She thought he was a natural and that he'd make a really great father. She'd never really thought about kids herself since her career had always been first priority. After being raised the way she had, she questioned if she would ever want kids.

"I moved a few things around, but the place is yours for as long as you need it."

"Thank you, Megan."

"Lacey came over and stocked the kitchen earlier. Robert agreed that the fewer people who know that you two are here, the better. If you need anything, just let us know. We can deliver meals, groceries, whatever. You can also call down to the restaurant and they will let Iian know what you want."

Rob sat back and listened quietly to them talking and tried to stifle another yawn.

"You must both be exhausted. I'll let you get some rest." She started to get up and Rob watched with slight amusement as it took her two tries to get out of the soft chair. Megan walked inside and came back out with a red key chain. "You know where everything is." She hugged Ric, who was standing, holding the little girl. "I'm so glad you're okay. Both of you." She smiled at them as she took her daughter from Ric.

Ric tossed both bags over his shoulder and they walked down a well-maintained pathway. Rob wasn't really a "nature" kind of girl, but she couldn't help but be impressed by the flowers and the beauty surrounding her. The tall trees provided shelter from the sun and lit the path with a soft, welcoming light. They'd passed a few small cabins, and when they reached another path that jutted off, they took it. She could see their cabin then. It was larger than the others and sat back by itself near a grove of trees. Three wooden steps led up to a large front porch, which overlooked the most breathtaking view of the ocean.

Rob had seen the Pacific before. For her tenth birthday, her dad had gotten an idea in his head and driven them to Seaside, Oregon. They had spent the whole day riding the bumper cars and eating junk food on the avenue. They'd walked away with great memories and several hundreds of dollars from other people's wallets. It had been the best day in her arsenal of childhood memories.

Ric set the bags down on the porch and crossed over to where she stood looking out at the view. His arms came around her and she leaned back into his chest.

"You should see it at sunset."

She closed her eyes, took a deep breath, and smelled ocean and clean air.

Katie Derby sat across from Jason and wondered why she had agreed to meet him at the coffee shop. She'd been embarrassed ever since Lynda's party several weeks ago where she had gotten drunk and admitted to him all the years of having feelings for him. Then she'd topped it off with a stupid kiss. One that he'd held still through, very still. It had been apparent to her that he didn't feel the same way about her. Now she sat fidgeting with her napkin in her lap, wishing to be anywhere else on the planet.

"It's not that…Well, it's just that…I had never…" He was mumbling, and she could tell he was terrified.

"Jason," she interrupted him, trying to explain before he said something that would rip her heart out. "I don't want you to think…well, I was very drunk. It was just a mistake. I don't want there to be any weirdness between us." A little part of her heart broke off and floated to the floor when he looked almost relieved.

Before he could respond, her cell phone rang. Seeing her brother's number, she hit ignore. Not two seconds later, it rang again. This time she saw her father's number and hit ignore as well.

Looking back at Jason, she noticed the fear in his eyes and could already tell the weirdness between them had settled in. She took a deep breath, but she wanted to pound her head on the table.

"Katie, I don't know…" Her phone rang again. Looking down she saw her mother's number.

"I'm sorry, Jason, I better…" she nodded to her phone.

"Sure." He looked like he wanted to bolt for the door.

"Hello, Mom, what's so important?" she answered, stepping away from the table and walking towards the back of the almost empty coffee shop.

"Katie, oh thank god you answered. I wanted to talk to you before you heard a bunch of lies from anyone else."

Her mother cleared her throat and then continued on. "Well, sweetie, first of all, I think you might have already heard from your brother that his apartment blew up. Don't worry, he wasn't in it and he's fine."

"What?" Katie tried to get more details, but her mother just continued talking.

"But I wanted to tell you something. I know it's going to come out very soon, and I thought you would want to hear the truth instead of the lies they are spreading on the news or hearing something completely false from the police."

Katie waited, knowing that she wouldn't be able to interrupt her mother once she got started.

"Twenty-six years ago, after your father and I had a huge falling out, I went to Italy to recover from my pain, and I had an affair with a man named Damiano Cardone. We had a son. I left them in Italy to come back and divorce your father, but he… well, we didn't get a divorce. Anyway, I kept in touch with them and in a roundabout way, Damiano and I are married. Well, that's not the important part. Four years later I visited them in Italy after your father was being difficult, and when I returned back home I realized I was pregnant again, and…well…this time I had you. Obviously, it was too late to keep it from your father since he had already found out I was pregnant. He was just so happy about it."

Katie felt herself starting to hyperventilate.

"I just couldn't break your father's heart, so I made him believe you were his. Damiano Cardone is your biological father, not Rodrick. I'm sorry I had to tell you over the…" Katie dropped her phone. Her ears were ringing and her vision grayed around the edges. Then Jason was beside her, yelling at her to breathe. The last thing she saw before she passed out was Jason's blue eyes, hovering over hers.

Ric let Roberta sleep as he made a few more calls using the cabin's phone. The first one was to his mother's cell phone. When he got her voice mail again, he left a vague message like the one he'd left the night before.

"Mom, I don't know if you listened to my message last night, or if you're on the way to Portland. Just don't go to my apartment, I'm not there. Actually, if you haven't already heard, my apartment isn't there anymore either, I'll be in touch with you when I can."

Then he called his sister. "Katie, I'll tell you what's going on later, I promise. I'm okay. Don't worry about me. I'm with Rob."

The last call was to his father. He'd called and left him

a message last night when he was at the station, telling him he was alive and well. He didn't usually talk to him this often, and when he did, it was usually uncomfortable. This time was going to be much worse than any other in the past.

Rodrick Stanton II had been raised in such lavishness that he demanded excellence from everyone around him, including his son, Rodrick Stanton III. Ric hated being called that. His father had almost had a stroke when, in junior high, he had started going by Ric instead of Rodrick.

His father answered the phone on the first ring. "What now, Kathleen?" He sounded annoyed.

"No, Dad, it's me." Ric didn't know that his parents had even been talking.

"Ric?" He heard the relief in his father's voice. "My god, son. Where are you? You've had your mother and I scared to death."

"Dad," he tried to cut in.

"We heard about your apartment exploding, then we don't hear a word from you, just quick voicemails. Those damn cops in Portland don't know a thing, either. Your mother is stuck on a long layover in New York and is calling me every two minutes."

"Dad." He waited until his father was quiet. "I'm okay. I'm sorry I didn't get a hold of you sooner. We've had some things to deal with here on this end, and I can't tell you where I am right now, but I can tell you I'm safe. I'll be off the grid for a few weeks until things settle down."

"What are you talking about?" His father sounded more annoyed than he'd ever heard before. He sighed then filled him in on every detail.

Less than an hour later, Ric stood over Rob. She'd fallen face down on the large bed still wearing all her clothes. It didn't appear that she'd moved at all in the last hour. Walking to the end of the bed, he gently removed her boots. She didn't budge.

Toeing off his own shoes, he stretched out next to her. There were two bedrooms in the cabin and he had it in his mind to only use one for their visit.

Everything had gone terribly wrong. Now he was another man down. He would have to hire some more pawns to do his bidding. He'd watched yesterday evening from down the street as Ric had exited the building and run right into the pretty detective's arms. Damn! The man was still alive and he'd failed at getting his revenge and getting his hands on her again.

He drove away slowly, thinking about his next move.

CHAPTER 15

*R*oberta felt pinned, and when she tried to move, something held her down. Opening one eye, she saw Ric's face next to hers. She knew where she was —she was in a small cabin somewhere along the coast of Oregon. She was also being smothered by a very large, very heavy man.

"Would you get off me?" she groaned. His legs had her pinned, and his arm was thrown over her chest, making it hard for her to breath.

When she tried to push him off, he snuggled in deeper, putting his nose into her neck. She laughed and shoved harder, but he was a solid wall. Then she noticed the smile on his face. "You think this is funny?" She rolled over and sat on him, pinning him down as she smiled down at him.

He laughed. "Okay, okay, I give up." He chuckled as she pinned his arms. Bending down to hold her face inches from his, she decided to enjoy herself.

She hadn't expected the slam of desire that quickly

spread through her. His mouth was warm and welcoming, and she took his bottom lip between her teeth and nibbled and sucked until he moaned. Then he tossed her around until their positions were reversed. Her breath was coming faster, and she could see the desire in his blue eyes, deepening the color.

"Ric," she whispered as he claimed her mouth.

"You're so soft," he said, running kisses down her jaw to feast on her neck just below her ear. She felt like her eyes were crossing. His mouth was spreading heat throughout her body. She arched up into his hands, which were running down her side. He reached just under her shirt, and she moaned when she felt his fingers play across her sensitive skin.

She pulled his shirt up and off and enjoyed the look of him as he hovered above her. She saw the two scars; the one on his shoulder was larger than the one on his side. He smiled as she ran her fingers over his tight chest. "Mmm." She licked her lips and he claimed her mouth again.

His hand continued on an upward motion until finally, she could feel it pulling down her silky bra. Then he was rolling her nipple between his fingers and she bucked underneath him.

"Please," she said against his mouth.

"God, I want you." He leaned down and pulled up her shirt, exposed her skin to his view. He took her breast into his mouth and sucked lightly, causing little bumps to rise on her skin and a moan to escape her lips.

She ran her hands over his arms and back and fisted a hand in his hair and just held on. He ran his hand over her stomach, lightly tracing circles as he feasted on her. Then he followed the downward path with his mouth. He ran his hand over her slacks, tugging them down and lightly touching the silk that covered her below. She moaned upon the featherlight contact.

"Beautiful," he said as he bent over her. "So soft." He ran kisses down the insides of her thighs, running his hands over her hips, over her ribs. He was touching her everywhere except the one place she needed him to. Then, when she felt she couldn't wait any longer, he touched her lightly through her silky underwear and she almost came right then.

She was wet and hot, waiting for his touch. When he did finally pull the silk aside, exposing her to him, she almost bucked off the bed.

He tugged her slacks further down her legs and pushed the small silky underwear down her legs all the way. His fingers played with her, causing her to let out a moan and close her eyes. His touch was so light, so warm, she didn't think she could take much more.

Then his mouth was on her and her hands went to his head, holding him where she wanted him. His fingers roamed her legs and hips gently. She enjoyed the feel of his calloused hands running over her skin. Closing her eyes on a moan, she felt him slip a finger into her and she almost came off the bed.

She didn't know how much more she could take.

"Ric."

"Shh, just let go," he whispered.

She did, and she screamed when the lights exploded behind her eyes while she convulsed into his mouth. She couldn't have controlled herself if she had tried.

~

Ric had never seen anything more beautiful than Roberta in the throes of ecstasy. Her face was flushed, her long dark hair was a jumbled mess spread out on the crisp white sheets, and her skin glowed. He lay there and held onto her until he could feel her breathing level.

"Mmm, thank you," she said against his bare chest.

He chuckled. "No, thank *you*." Just then he heard her stomach let out a loud growl and he laughed.

"I guess we'd better go see what there is in the kitchen."

She looked at him with concern. "Didn't you... Don't you..." Was she actually blushing?

"Later. We have time. I think we both need some food and maybe a shower." He kissed her nose. "Why don't you jump in the shower while I try to find something decent to eat?"

Twenty minutes later, he sat on the front deck watching the seagulls and enjoying the sights and sounds of the evening. There was a light breeze coming from the water. It was about an hour from sunset, but even now, the sky was filled with wonderful hues.

He looked up and saw Rob walk out the front door. Her long hair was wet, and he liked the way it curled lightly around her face. She wore a tan pair of shorts and a blue top with a light brown jacket over it. Her feet were bare, and she looked like she belonged on the beach.

"I whipped up some scrambled eggs and toast. If we want anything more elaborate, we'll need to make a list for Megan." She sat next to him on the bench.

"It looks wonderful." She smiled over at him. He could see the concentration on her face.

"I need to deal with…"

"Tomorrow," he said and took a bite of his toast.

"But—" she started to say. He just looked up at her.

"We can deal with all that tomorrow. This is Pride, not Portland. Everything moves more slowly around here, you'll see. Besides, it's almost eight, and I doubt you'd get the local sheriff on the phone. He's probably home watching a ball game by now."

They sat on the deck and ate their toast with eggs while watching the sun sink lower over the Pacific Ocean.

Heading to the shower himself, he left Roberta to enjoy the sunset. He'd been lucky to have his bag in the trunk of his car. He had an extra suit, which he wouldn't need in the next few weeks that they were going to be in Pride. He was happy to discover a razor and his extra gym clothes, as well as an older pair of jeans and three extra shirts. He supposed it could have been worse. He thought of when Allison's house had burned down almost two years ago, and she'd lost everything.

It wasn't like he was homeless like she had been. He still had his three thousand square foot apartment in Los Angeles.

He appreciated Megan and Todd helping them out. Since he'd first met them, he'd had nothing but the highest respect for them and the small town they lived in. He visited frequently.

Actually, he'd enjoyed his time here so much, he had at one point thought about buying a place here to spend his downtime. Maybe someplace overlooking the beach, like Allison and Iian's house did.

Allison had been his greatest find. The fact that Megan had actually discovered Allison's wonderful artistic talent didn't stop him from claiming her as his own. He gave Megan props for finding her, but it was thanks to his talent and hard work that she was now one of the most well-known names in the art world. Ally was not only a great artist, she was his friend. When she'd lived above his studio a few years back, they'd become close. He loved and respected her as a person and an artist, something he never thought he'd be able to say. Most of the artists he worked with were moody, self-absorbed snobs that thought they were better than they actually were.

He thought about Sandi, the young artist that he was trying to sign, and wondered if the girl was alright. He didn't like leaving when everything was still up in the air with her. He didn't even know where she was or if she was safe.

Allison had helped him realize not every artist was created equal. Ric looked forward to seeing Allison and Iian's new son, Conner, again. He'd visited last summer right after Allison had given birth. The small bundle had reminded him so much of Iian, he'd sworn they'd just cloned him. He laughed now remembering how proud the man had been.

Since that day, he'd been wondering about kids himself. He hadn't planned on a family. To be honest, he'd gone through the last ten years avoiding any deep relationships.

After all, his parents weren't the best role models. Now, with the news of his mother's infidelity, he wondered if he could ever maintain a stable relationship with anyone.

Then he remembered the glow of Roberta under him and he ached for her.

"What the hell do you mean he's dead?" he heard Rob saying as he walked out of the shower with a towel wrapped around his waist. She looked over at him and he thought he saw a flash of desire cross her eyes.

"Fine, I'll talk to you tomorrow. Yeah, okay, give me the details then." She pushed the button hard on the untraceable cell phone they were to use.

"Who's dead?"

"Robbie Bender." She tossed the phone down on the couch and started to pace the floor. "Apparently, he was stabbed twenty times in his cell." She turned and looked at him. "What the hell is going on? Is there something you're not telling me?" She approached him and pointed a finger in his chest. "Who have you pissed off?"

He just looked at her, wondering this himself.

She turned and started to pace again. "This person has either power or a lot of money. First, Kenny Sorvillo ends up floating down the Columbia. Then they hire Ricky Scoles to grab me. Why? Why me?" She shook her head. "Now Robbie Bender ends up with a shiv sticking out of his back." She continued to pace and stare off into space.

Deciding she needed to wind down, he stepped in front of her.

"Put it away for now." He pulled her close. Her hair was still damp from her shower. He could smell her sweet scent and wanted to taste her again.

"You're still wet." She pulled back, looking up into his eyes, and he watched as she licked her lips as her eyes ran over him.

Then she was shoving him back against the wall and her mouth was on his. She moved like the wind, fast and dangerous. She tasted like warm summer nights with a hint of exotic flowers, and she filled his senses completely. He reversed their positions and held her against the wall, running his hands up and down her body. Her shorts were tight and he enjoyed playing his hands over her tight rear end as he deepened the kiss.

She too ran her hands over him and he loved feeling her fingers run up and down his bare back and arms.

He pushed her up and she wrapped one leg around his hip as he held her against the wall. He heard a moan escape her lips. Walking them back a few steps to their room, he managed to turn their bodies and he landed on his back as they fell onto the bed. He ran his hands lower and quickly unsnapped her shorts, pulling them down and off in one fluid motion.

He rolled over, losing his towel in the process. Now they were both naked and the skin-on-skin sensation was almost overwhelming. She was softer than he could have ever imagined. Her shorter frame was just right, and her curves caused him so much pleasure. He ran his mouth down her long neck and she wrapped her legs around his hips so their cores touched.

"Here, let me just..." He reached over and removed a condom from the nightstand. He'd come prepared and was thankful.

As he came back down to her, she arched upwards. "Now...please..." She moved until he was poised at her entrance. "I need you now, Ric." She wrapped a leg around his calf.

Looking down into her face as he entered her slowly,

he saw her eyes cloud over. Her legs were wrapped around his hips and she was holding onto him tightly. He moved slowly at first, building the anticipation, then he lost track and lost himself in the feel of her. She was tight and warm, and she wrapped around him perfectly. He tried everything to hold out, to hold on until he heard her and felt her convulse around him. Then he moved more quickly, taking his pleasure harder and faster until he convulsed inside, then collapsed on top of her.

"I meant to go slower," he chuckled into her hair a few minutes later.

"Why? I wouldn't have changed a thing." She was playing her hand over his back. "I really like your butt. I mean, most men have okay asses, but yours…" She ran her hand over him and squeezed a little. "I mean, how did you get such a fine backside?"

He pulled back and looked down at her with a grin. Her face was flushed, her hair was fanned out on the pillow, and her lips were swollen from his kisses. He could feel himself hardening inside her again. He could just imagine spending the next few weeks in this bed with her.

She moved her hips and he closed his eyes on a moan. "You like that?" she whispered. "How about this?" She twisted a little.

"Roberta…" He leaned down and kissed her mouth again, showing her the hunger that was in him.

The way he was holding himself above her, she had to do something quickly to get him moving. The fire he'd started had yet to be extinguished completely. Bending down, she rubbed her tongue over his flat nipple and ran kisses along his collarbone. His chest was wide and covered in a light dusting of blond hair. His pecs were just as marvelous as his butt. His arms were strong, and his lean muscles called to be licked. Pushing on his left shoulder, she forced him to reverse their positions.

Giving his body her full attention, she ran her hand and mouth over the length of his upper torso, slowing only when he moaned so she could give better attention to the areas she knew he enjoyed. She'd never seen a six-pack on a man before. She'd been with other men over the years—she wasn't one to deny her sexual desires—but none of them had looked like Ric: tall, lean, tan, and full of muscles. His thighs were spread wide as she sat between them, playing her hands up and down his lightly hairy legs.

"You must run a lot," she said nibbling on his thigh, causing him to moan again.

"I try to every…" She didn't give him a chance to finish. Her tongue darted out and licked the length of him. He bucked and grabbed her head. Pulling her hair aside, he watched her as she lowered her head and took him fully into her mouth.

She was lost in the enjoyment of pleasing him. She watched him throw back his head and saw the veins in his neck bulge.

Sliding up his body, she rubbed her chest against his stomach and licked her way back up to his mouth. "You taste so good, mmm."

She reached over and grabbed another condom, and this time she took the time to put it on him herself. He watched her with desire in his eyes. She moved up to her knees and positioned him just right so when she slid down slowly, she was fully impaled and could feel him filling her completely. His hands came to her hips and he held her still. Then she moved a little and, throwing her head back, she grabbed his hands and held on until they were both breathless and sated.

CHAPTER 16

*T*he next day the sheriff stopped by to visit them. Sheriff Robert Brogan was younger than Roberta had imagined, and he had a very friendly face. He was short but well-built and looked like he knew what he was doing. With most cops, Rob could tell if they fit the job. Brogan fit.

He gave them his contact numbers for emergencies and assured them he would call if he or anyone else saw anybody new in town. He appeared more relaxed than any other cop Rob had ever worked with outside of Portland, and she liked the man quite a bit.

That evening, Rob walked with Ric along the beach. The next morning, she jogged with him along the same path and quickly decided she needed to run with him more often. He pushed her to maintain her speed, and she could tell he'd slowed down for her sake, which just made her want to get up to speed faster.

They'd maintained phone silence as per the commander's request, never answering any business or personal calls on their private phones. So far Katie hadn't called, but Rob knew that Ric had watched for her call.

Ric had his guard down and looked and acted totally relaxed, but Rob knew that she couldn't afford to drop her guard. In fact, she still carried her service weapon strapped to her back everywhere they went.

She met Todd, Megan's husband when he delivered their dinner their second night there. He'd brought some more groceries that they'd requested, as well.

Todd was as tall as Ric and had dark brown wavy hair and silvery, blue eyes that matched his son's eyes. Matthew was a mini version of his father, right down to the small cleft in his chin. She had been instantly charmed by the pair.

The following night it was his brother, Iian, who had delivered their dinner from his restaurant, The Golden Oar. She could tell they were brothers instantly. Iian had half a foot of height on his brother, and he also had a wider chest and arms, but the silver eyes, dark curly hair, and the small cleft in his chin had also been present. She'd yet to meet their sister, Lacey, and wondered if she too had these traits.

Iian had been deaf since a boating accident at age eighteen, and since Rob had a limited knowledge of sign language, Ric had translated their conversations. She only knew a little of the alphabet and a few cuss words she'd learned around the station, so for the most part, she just sat back and watched the two men enjoy a quiet conversation.

Iian had been eager to show off his new son, Conner. He told them that Allison was working—she was an art teacher at the school—but assured them that she would stop by later the next evening for dinner at Megan's. Lacey and Aaron were supposed to be there with their daughter, Lilly, as well.

Roberta was curious to meet Allison and Lacey; she'd heard a lot about the two women since arriving in Pride.

She remembered seeing pictures of Ric and Allison together and tried to hide the jealousy that surfaced. She wasn't the jealous type; at least she'd never had any cause to be so in the past.

Looking over at Ric as they walked along the shoreline now, she felt her hand in his and smiled.

He'd shown her such gentleness the last two days and she was beginning to relax. She'd never had a time in her life like this when she could relax her guard a little. Her life with her father, then with the gang, and finally with the police, had always kept her on her toes. She could get used to the slower pace.

They reached a small bluff and he turned her to face him.

"There's something I've been meaning to talk to you about." He looked so serious. "I talked to my mother shortly before...well...everything exploded, so to speak." He tried for a smile, but it hadn't reached his eyes. She tilted her head and waited.

"She confirmed that Dante is my half-brother and that Katie is actually my half-sister." She saw the anger in his eyes and the hurt.

Her mind was spinning in a new direction. "Ric, this changes things."

"What do you mean?" He released her hand.

"You're telling me Dante Cardone, owner of New Edges, one of the largest, most influential and wealthy businesses in Portland, is your half-brother." He nodded his head, "Did it ever occur to you that he could be behind all this?" She started walking back towards the cabin and the phone.

"Hold on a second." He spun her around, holding her shoulders so she would stay put. "I've checked the man out thoroughly and if he was behind this, I would know."

"That's bullshit." She tried to pull away.

"This is a police matter. You should have told me the second you confirmed it. I know we talked about it, but you should have told me. At least you should have told me the night after your apartment blew up in your face." She pulled away and started to pace. "We knew he might be, but this confirmation changes everything." She started to walk to the cabin again. "I have to call it in."

He followed her in silence as she marched back up the beach. She could tell he was mad, but she didn't care at this point. With something this big, did he know that he'd kept them in danger? If Dante Cardone was behind this, he could have been put behind bars by now, and they could be safe.

Several hours later, she finally hung up the phone from the many calls she'd made. She itched to get back to Portland to be the one to interview the man.

They had brought Dante in for questioning and he'd immediately contacted his lawyers and had a team of them in the interview room. Apparently, Ric's mother, Kathleen, had been staying at his place and had followed him down to the station, demanding to know what was going on with her son. Less than an hour later, they'd released Dante with no new answers. His lawyers had been that good.

Ric had quietly sat and listened to her side of the conversations. She could see he was keeping his temper at bay. When he'd heard his mother's name, he had gone pale. Now, however, he walked over and picked up the cell phone and punched in a number.

"Hi, yeah. I know. Yeah." He listened, and Roberta could hear a woman's voice on the other end. "I know, Mom." He turned his back on Roberta and walked out the front door and shut it behind him. When she heard the door click shut, a little part of her closed.

She was a fool! What was she doing getting involved with someone from a case? She closed her eyes and let out a breath, not realizing that tears slid down her face. Walking into the restroom, she closed the door and looked at herself in the mirror.

What did he see in her? She was short and plain looking. Her nose was a little crooked from one of the many blows from her father. She thought the hazel in her eyes was ordinary. She did like the way her hair hung in long curls down her back; she'd always thought it was her best feature. When she was younger, her father had always made her wear it short, in case it should get caught on something during a get-a-way. After becoming a detective, she'd grown it out and had enjoyed it ever since.

She knew Ric's type—tall, blonde, gorgeous. Now she'd gone and messed everything up. She knew she was a little rough around the edges. Most of the men she'd dated had complained that she was emotionless. Watching the light tears seep down her cheeks, she dashed them away quickly. Why did it matter so much to her what Ric thought of her? She had never cried over someone before.

This was her job, and she had done the right thing. He'd hindered her investigation by not providing the necessary information. Her job was to protect him. Period. Not sleep with him.

Taking a large cleansing breath, she dashed cold water on her face and tied her hair back in her standard braid. Stepping back into her professional mindset, she walked back out, feeling almost under control again.

Later, they walked to Megan's house in silence and she was introduced to everyone else. Allison Jordan had surprised her. She'd seen pictures of the woman and had thought she was beautiful, but she was more beautiful in person. Nothing compared to the fit of jealousy she felt when she saw Ric kiss and hug the woman. She noticed Iian, Allison's husband, standing back and smiling at her, and she felt embarrassed, knowing he had seen what was in her eyes.

Lacey was delightful. She was a perfect package and looked a lot like the woman in one of Allison's paintings, which hung in their cabin. She carried the family eyes that seemed to see right through Roberta's shield. Her husband, Aaron, had made her feel welcomed. He had blond hair and warm eyes and had held on tight to their daughter, Lilly, who looked to be a great mix of her parents. She had to admit, being in a room full of truly beautiful people made her feel dull and plain.

She was still so charmed by little Matthew with his dark messy hair and the cleft in his chin, which had melted her heart earlier. The little girls in their little dresses were adorable, but something about seeing the little man in his school uniform and shirt and tie did something to her.

Everyone talked loudly and sat comfortably at the table like they did this every day. She realized she was so out of her league; she'd never even sat down for a family dinner before in her life. Did they notice that she didn't know how to act? Looking over at Ric, she saw him looking right at home bouncing little Sara on his knee. He belonged here; she didn't.

~

Ric sat at Megan's large dining room table across from Rob and wondered what she was thinking. The place was filled with people and was very noisy, yet she sat there with her "cop mask" on. She smiled at everyone and made small talk, but he could see the dullness in her eyes. The sparkle he'd seen in them the last couple of days was gone, and he wanted nothing more than to see it there again.

The conversation with his mother had been hard. The call he'd received from his father had been even harder. He still hadn't talked to his sister and wondered where she was. He'd tried several times to call her before coming to dinner with no success. He was beginning to worry.

It felt like his family was falling apart. But he was sitting in a large room filled with people he liked and respected, and he tried to enjoy their company.

Allison and Iian's son, Conner, was a gem. Less than a year old, the little guy would laugh and smile when he held him and tickled his chubby cheeks. Lacey and Aaron's little girl was beyond cute as she walked around, falling on her padded bottom a lot. Then there were Megan's two kids. Being surrounded by all these kids really made him realize what he'd been missing. Not only did he want what they had, he knew who he wanted it with. And, right now, she didn't look too pleased with him.

After dinner, they walked back to the cabin in silence.

He'd reached for her hand only to have her pull it away a few steps later.

When they reached the cabin, she walked towards the second bedroom. He followed her and was amused as she tried to shut the door behind her. He flung it open before she could flip the small lock on the handle.

"Okay, what's this all about?" He stood in the doorway and crossed his arms and watched as she stood there and tried to look authoritative.

"We both know it's not going to go anywhere."

"What isn't going to go anywhere?" He watched anger cross her face. He started to walk towards her. She held her hands up trying to block him.

"This." She waved a hand between them. "I need to step back. I'm here to protect—"

"Screw that," he burst in. When she started to speak again, he continued. "No, you'll listen to me now. I just had what can only be described as the worst conversations ever with my parents. I'm worried sick that my sister might have found out…" He broke off and looked at her face. Taking a deep breath, he admitted, "I'm worried sick that my baby sister might have found out that she doesn't belong to my father. That she is just my half-sister and that she has a full brother out there and a father that she's never even met." He ran his hands through his hair and walked into the living room. The walls of the bedroom were closing in on him.

Roberta came up behind him and put her arms around him. He hadn't known the fear would show that much. Closing his eyes, he leaned back into her.

"I'm sorry, I really like Katie a lot. Just because

someone else might be her father doesn't diminish the fact that you're her brother.

"I know. Todd is Lacey and Iian's half-brother, and they don't even acknowledge it." He turned and pulled her into his arms. "Why are you upset?"

"Ric, I can't get involved. I shouldn't get involved."

"Why?" He pulled her face up to his.

She closed her eyes and tried to pull away, but he held her in place.

"Why, Roberta? Why can't you get involved? Don't tell me it's because of the job. I won't buy it."

Resting her head on his shoulder, she opened up to him.

"I was raised by my father, a thief, and I was lucky to go a month without bruises somewhere from him. He taught me to be a thief, as well. When my father died of a heart attack when I was sixteen, I was on my own. I couldn't even bury him. I had to just leave him on the street because I was afraid the cops would find out I was on my own and put me in a home." She didn't realize tears were rolling down her face until he quietly wiped them away.

"Then there was the gang. They were my pseudo-family until they were gunned down right in front of me." She pulled away and looked at him. "I can't get close. I won't…"

"I won't leave. I'm not going to go anywhere." He could see her reasoning now, and he bent and kissed her mouth softly. "Don't push me away because you're afraid. I won't be scared off that easily." He pulled her closer and could feel her softening.

"I haven't been in a relationship like this before, Ric. I'm afraid I'm no good at it."

"Neither have I, but I'm willing to try if you are." He smiled at her, pulling her up onto her toes as he kissed her mouth and started walking her back towards their room.

She laughed when he picked her up and walked her the rest of the way with her feet dangling. Tossing her down lightly on the bed he said, "Good. Now that our first fight is over, we can move on to the make-up sex."

Pulling his shirt over his head, he tossed it aside.

"That was not a fight," she said, and he watched her eyes travel up and down his bare chest.

Smiling, even more, he said, "You next."

She sat up and removed her shirt and smiled in return. Then he unbuckled the snap of his jeans. She mimicked him with her pants. His zipper was next, then hers. Pulling his jeans down, he watched as she followed the motion slowly, sliding her pants off her legs and finally tossing them aside. He stood there at the end of the bed in his boxers and looked at her in her pink bra and panties.

"You're beautiful." His mouth went dry as she ran her hands slowly up her sides and over her breasts. He didn't move when her hands skimmed back down and played just outside her panties, rubbing her fingers over her softness. He watched in awe as she toyed with herself, smiling at him. When he moved to get closer, she shook her head.

"No, you started this game. Just watch me." She leaned back and pulled her bra loose, rolling her nipples between her fingers. He stood by, his mouth dry, his palms sweaty, as hard as stone.

"Watch what you do to me, what I want you to do to me." Her voice was husky and rich and he wanted to claim her mouth. Then she pushed her panties aside and ran her fingers over her pink skin underneath as he moaned.

"Touch yourself, Ric. I want to see what I do to you." She smiled when he yanked his boxers down quickly.

"This." He pointed to his hard-on. "You do this." He wanted her.

When he went to move again, she said. "No, show me."

He felt stupid standing at the end of the bed touching himself, but then she slid a finger into herself and he didn't care anymore. Her eyes closed on a soft moan and her head tilted back.

Did she know how wonderful she looked? The evening sun was lighting up the room, casting pink shadows across her skin and it looked radiant, she looked radiant. Looking at her face, he realized she'd been watching him as he followed the motion of her fingers, matching them with his own hand. He wanted her so badly now, and he could see that she wanted him too. Her fingers were slick, and he could smell the sweetness of her excitement. Then in one quick motion, he was on the bed and he thrust himself inside her heat as she screamed out his name.

CHAPTER 17

*T*he phone rang, and Ric sat up, squinting at the clock. It was a quarter past one in the morning. Not wanting to take the chance of missing a call from Katie, he sprinted across the room, hitting his shin on the edge of the bed in the process. He looked at the screen and answered when he saw his sister's picture on the screen.

"Hello." He cleared his throat.

"Ric…" His sister's voice sounded small.

"Katie, my god. I've been so worried. Where are you?"

"Is it true?" She sounded like she'd been crying. Obviously, she'd heard the news.

"I'm so sorry. I didn't expect you to find out like this. Who told you?"

"Mom called me." He heard her sniffle.

"Have you talked to Dad yet?" When she heard the word "Dad," she laughed. "Katie, he's still your father. I'm still your brother. He loves you, I love you."

"Ric, I don't know what to do, what to say. I can't talk to him right now, and I won't talk to her."

"Where are you?" he asked again.

"At a friend's. I'm going to drop off for a while. I need to settle some things."

"Why don't I—"

"No, Ric. I just need some time. I'll call you when I can." It was quiet, and Ric waited. "I'm glad you're okay. I'm sorry about your apartment. You scared me; don't do it again. I love you, Ric." He heard the click and just continued to hold the phone to his ear as he stared out into the darkness outside the cabin windows.

How could his mother do this? Why would she do something so mean as to tell her over the phone? Did she have no heart? He tossed the phone across the room.

He felt Roberta's arms wrap around him from behind.

"She told her over the phone." The more he thought about it, the angrier he got. "She couldn't even face her when she ripped out her heart. Just like she did to my father, to me." He spun around. "What kind of heartless bitch tells her daughter over the phone that she has a different father than the man who raised her and loved her as his own?" He paced the small room as she watched him in silence.

"Maybe it *is* better to not get involved with someone. After all, my father gave over thirty years to her. Twenty-six of them, she spent lying to him and married to another man across the world, while raising another family." He wanted to punch something.

"Ric—"

"Don't!" He turned, but she didn't back down from his anger. She had told him where she'd come from and about the years of abuse from her father. He thought she would flinch when he approached her, but instead, she stood tall and didn't even blink. That made him want her even more, and he yanked her off her feet and kissed her hard. He wanted her hot, fast, and hard. He needed it.

He knew he was bruising her lips under his own. He fisted his hands in her hair and yanked her head back, exposing her neck. Running his mouth down, he nibbled and sucked harder than he meant to. The pain in his heart was reflected in his actions. When she moaned and pushed her hands into his hair, he spun her around and shoved her up against the wall. He didn't want her to want him. He wanted to fill his need, only his need.

How could he know that by taking his pleasure, he was giving it to her in return? It was primal, something inside him called to take what he wanted, quickly.

He yanked her tight shorts down and had his fingers deep inside her, more roughly than he'd expected. She moaned and leaned her forehead against the wall, placing both her hands on the wall. When he pushed her faster, farther, she tossed her head back on a moan.

Then he moved her legs farther apart, moving her closer to the wall, trapping her hands between them. Using his feet, he spread her legs even wider and entered her fast. His long, hard thrusts matched his tension and desires. He kissed the back of her neck and lightly bit her ear, causing her to almost scream in delight. Letting lose his control, he kept the speed fast and the thrusts long and hard as he took her quickly against the wall, her hair fisted in his hands as he ravished her neck and listened to her moaning his name.

He'd built himself up so tight that when he did come, he growled out her name and felt his legs weaken.

"I'm sorry," he said into her hair a few minutes after he'd gained control of himself again. He held her up against the wall, not wanting to move. He was afraid of what he'd see in her face. Had he hurt her? He could feel her breathing hard against his chest.

Turning in his arms, she looked at him and saw what he'd been trying to hide from her.

"Don't." She grabbed his face and held it so he looked at her. "If I hadn't wanted to be up against the wall, I wouldn't have been. I can take care of myself, Ric. I'm not some fragile flower who doesn't want hot, fastsex, standing up."

He laughed and pulled her closer, smelling her hair.

"Regardless, I should have gotten myself under control first."

"I'll let you in on a little secret," she whispered into his ear. "You can lose control like that on me any day."

The next few days were a blur. They walked on the beach and ate dinner either at the cabin or at Megan's house. Once they took a walk down the beach all the way to Allison and Iian's house, which was triple the size of Megan and Todd's place.

Roberta was beginning to think everyone lived the high life in this small town. Allison had shown Ric some of her latest paintings, and they'd ended up talking shop for several hours while little Conner had napped. She enjoyed this side of Ric. He seemed more relaxed talking shop with Allison. He'd quickly marked the paintings he'd wanted her to ship to his offices, though he'd picked almost everything. There was a small piece she'd seen leaning against the wall that caught Roberta's eye and she was studying it when Allison walked up behind her.

"He makes for a good subject, doesn't he?" Rob had jumped, not knowing Allison was behind her.

"Hmm." She tilted her head and studied it further.

"You can have it if you want." Allison walked over and handed her the small sketch.

"Oh, no, I couldn't."

"Please, consider it a gift for saving my friend's life." Rob looked into Allison's eyes and saw the kindness there.

Looking down at the sketch of Ric, she held out her hands and Allison placed the small picture in them.

"I've got the perfect frame." She rushed to the other side of the room. "Here it is." Walking back, she took the sketch and put it inside the black-matted frame, which enhanced the drawing.

Looking around the room, she noticed Ric smiling back at her.

"Thank you. Now I have something to throw darts at when he acts up." Everyone laughed.

"What do you want to do today?" Ric asked. They were sitting on the front deck eating their breakfast of homemade cinnamon rolls that Lacey had delivered less than a half hour ago. They sat on the deck and watched the summer rain pelting the beach.

She'd been thinking about it for a few days. It was only

a short three-hour drive; they could be back just after dark. But she hadn't mentioned it to Ric out of fear. Fear that he'd talk her into visiting her grandparents; fear about the possibility of meeting her mother.

"I know it's far-fetched, but I've thought about driving into Cathlamet, Washington, to go by where my grandparents lived. Maybe see if I can find them. I have the address that was listed when I was abducted by my father, but I'm not sure if they still live—"

"That sounds like a wonderful idea. I'd love to go for a drive." He smiled over at her and took her hand in his.

They packed up some sandwiches for the drive and, after checking herself in the mirror at least three times, she decided she looked good enough for the possibility of meeting her family, people she had never known, and who had no idea that today, their lives might change drastically.

The three-hour drive was peaceful. The summer rain had let up just as they hit Astoria. They stopped in a large park along the water's edge and ate their packed lunches. Ric tossed a few bread crumbs to some seagulls, which only caused a huge surge of new birds to flock in their direction. Rob snapped a picture of him with her cell phone as he was laughing at a bird taking a potato chip from his fingers.

When he started to drive across the Astoria bridge, she could see his knuckles whiten from the death grip on the steering wheel.

"Afraid of bridges?" she joked.

"No, just heights."

She laughed again, "Afraid of heights? A man who had an apartment on the twentieth floor is afraid of heights."

She saw him relax a little when the bridge dipped down to water level.

An hour later, they rolled into the small town of Cathlamet. Like Pride, it sat on the waterfront, but instead of the Pacific, the wide, busy Columbia River was its port.

"Here's the address. It shouldn't be too hard to find." She could feel the nerves building in her. Only once in her life had she felt this nervous? When her father had died, she'd had a full-on panic attack not knowing what was going to happen to her.

They drove through the small town, past quaint rows of houses. Ric turned onto the street and immediately they started climbing up a steep hill. They followed the winding road until they came to a cluster of houses. He slowed down and when she spotted the number, she held her breath as he came to a stop in front of the small wood-framed house with a red roof.

There were potted plants on the small front porch, so many that it looked like a jungle. Flowers of every color bloomed in the warm summer sun. A "Welcome" sign hung on the front glass door. The yard was well maintained, and she could tell that whoever lived here took care of the place.

"Well?" Ric leaned over and brushed her hair back.

"Yeah, well." Taking a deep breath, she started to open her door.

They walked up the sidewalk in silence, and it took ringing the door twice to finally get a response.

"Coming." She heard a woman's voice from the back of the house.

Through the glass, she could see a woman who appeared to be in her late sixties walking towards them.

She was wiping her hands on a dish towel and looking at them cautiously.

When she opened the door, her eyes were on Ric, but when she started speaking, she looked over to Rob.

"Can I help you…" She broke off mid-sentence and her hand went to her heart, and for a minute, Rob was concerned she'd just had a stroke. Her face went white, her eyes blinked several times, and her mouth fell open.

Ric stepped in and gently took the woman's arm. "Here now, are you alright?" He started to walk the woman to a large chair that sat in the front room. The woman kept her eyes focused on Rob's face.

"Do you want some water?" Ric was leaning over the woman who was now sitting in the chair. Her hands still clenched the towel over her heart.

"Who?" She looked at Ric briefly. "Who are you?"

"I'm Roberta Stanton, this is Ric Derby. I'm sorry to bother you, ma'am. May I sit?" Rob's hands were sweaty. When the woman nodded, Rob took a seat across the room and Ric walked over and sat next to her, taking her hand in his.

"Stanton, Stanton. Your father was he…" Rob could see the wheels turning.

"My father's name was Robert Stanton. At least, that's the name he went by. Are you Eliza Catalonia?"

Rob could see some similarities, but she wanted to make sure. She needed the confirmation.

"How old are you?" the woman asked, not answering her question.

"I'll be twenty-eight in October."

Upon this news, the woman's face lit up and tears started slowly flowing down her cheeks.

"You're Ruth Ann, aren't you?"

Ruth Ann. The name was so wholesome sounding to Rob. She couldn't imagine what her life would have been like as Ruth Ann.

"I believe so, yes."

CHAPTER 18

*T*hey sat in the living room looking at each other, then the woman, Eliza, quickly excused herself and rushed to grab her phone and make a quick call. She came back into the room with more tears in her eyes.

"I wish Steven was alive to see you." She patted her eyes with the hand towel. "He died almost seven years ago. An accident at the plant he worked in across the river. We looked everywhere for you. After…" She sat and just looked at Rob's face, taking in every inch.

"I knew it when I first saw you. You look like your mother and brother. Oh!" She jumped up and went to grab the phone again. "One more call." She held up her hand.

Less than an hour later, Rob and Ric sat in a room full of people they didn't know, but that Rob was definitely related to. Rob's mother, Maria, looked so much like Rob, at first Ric thought they could be sisters.

When Rob's brother, Ethan, walked in less than fifteen minutes later, he immediately saw the resemblance. The man was taller at just over six foot, and he had an impressive amount of muscle. He wore his military fatigues. Ric noticed that he didn't relax the entire time they were there and that he hadn't seemed overly surprised to see his sister, like the others, had.

They met Rob's stepfather, Ken. Apparently, he and Rob's mother lived just a few miles down the road. Ethan was stationed up north, near Seattle, and had just been down for the weekend, visiting.

"You must stay for dinner. Oh no, you must stay for the night," Eliza was saying.

Looking over to Rob, he nodded his head in agreement. How could they leave? She looked like she was truly enjoying herself. Her initial nerves were gone, replaced with curiosity and excitement.

It was just after dinner when Rob's brother pulled her aside. It was weird knowing she had a half-brother; it was weirder looking into his eyes and seeing her own staring back at her.

He pulled her onto the back deck where it was darker. Somehow, the darkness suited him better than the bright lights of the kitchen. Rob stared at his features, so much like her own, but different.

"I'm glad you found them." He nodded his head towards the loud house where her family was celebrating her return. "Ruth...Roberta," he corrected, "there's something I need to tell you." He started pacing, then turned back to her. "I found you." He took a deep breath.

When she just looked at him with a confused look, he continued. "I found you over a month ago. I was in Portland for a…anyway, I was in Portland and I saw you at the hospital. You were there with your friend." He nodded his head towards the glass doors. She looked and saw Ric standing there laughing at something her mother was saying. "I knew who you were in an instant. I followed you, found out who you were and left something for you to…"

"The medallion! You left it in my apartment. Why? Why did my father have it?"

"Yes, I left it knowing you'd start looking into your family. The medallions have been handed down for many generations. I couldn't get in contact with you then…" He looked like he wanted to say more but couldn't. "I knew you would find them, find us." He smiled for the first time and his whole face changed. He looked kinder, more relaxed. She knew some military types took being serious to new levels, and he was one of those types.

"Mom said that hers went missing the night you disappeared, and I knew that you would have it. I can't stay tonight, but I wanted you to know that I'm glad you're here for them." He was looking into the house towards his family, their family. "I'll be gone for a while, overseas. It'll be hard on them."

"Don't worry, I have a feeling that now that they know who and where I am, I'll be seeing a lot more of them from here on out." Rob smiled. "You know, I've always wanted a baby sister. But I guess a brother will have to do."

They laughed and hugged for the first time.

~

Ric watched from inside the house as Rob and her brother hugged. He liked to think he knew her pretty well by now, but she amazed him with her relaxed attitude about everything. Maybe she'd had enough time to settle it all in her mind before meeting these people. Watching Rob and Ethan walk in the back door together made him think of his own family, how torn it was right now, how screwed up it felt. Would they ever be at a place where everyone was okay again?

Knowing that Rob's family was just as messed up as his, and yet was able to laugh and rejoice at the return of a long-lost family member, gave him hope.

Would he embrace his half-brother the same way he had just watched Rob hold onto hers? Somehow, he doubted it. Then he thought of Katie and his happy mood soured even more. He knew she'd asked for time to heal, but he was having a hard time letting her go.

Rob stepped up to him just then. "Deep thoughts?" She smiled and wrapped her arms around him.

Shaking his head clear, he kissed the top of her head. "I like your family."

"Mmm, I'm beginning to as well."

They slept in a guest room down the hallway from her grandmother's room. Ric held her in his arms and stared at the ceiling until sleep finally came.

The next morning, after having one of the largest breakfast they'd ever eaten, they headed back to Pride. Rob's grandmother and mother had cried, and they'd taken more than a dozen photos of Rob with everyone. They'd even snapped a few of Rob and Ric.

The drive back to Pride was a quiet one; he could tell she was on an emotional high. She kept looking at her phone, where she had a few dozen photos of them.

"Do you remember what I said back at your gallery that night?"

He looked over at her; she was looking at a picture of her and her brother.

"That you're glad you were raised by your father, that you wouldn't be who you were without him."

She nodded her head. "I guess that still rings true, but after meeting them…" She trailed off.

"Rob, I know this is hard, and they seem like very nice people. I just can't imagine you there, with them. Look at who you are…"

"No, that's not it." She looked up at him, and then he saw the tears. "After meeting them, I think I can truly appreciate where I come from now. If I had been raised there, with them, I don't think I could have become who I am now. I probably would have married young and had a passel of kids by now. Who knows, maybe I'd be two-hundred pounds and do nothing but watch soap operas all day."

He laughed at the thought. "No, you wouldn't."

"Well, maybe not watch soap operas." She laughed along with him.

Where were they? The dark man knew they'd gone off together, but he didn't know where. He had several new men out looking for them and it was costing him plenty.

He had a guy keeping track of their cell phone calls, but nothing had turned up so far.

He'd even driven by her place himself several times. Knowing it was just a matter of time before they'd slip up, he felt he could wait patiently to get his hands on her. Dealing with Ric was a different matter. He wanted the man taken care of, and the sooner the better. He had a score to settle and he didn't want it hanging over his head much longer.

A few days after their trip to Cathlamet, Rob received the call from her commander telling her they'd caught José. He'd broken into Rob's apartment and had started trashing the place. He claimed he was looking for information on her whereabouts. He was currently in the holding cell under tight guard.

"Rob, he claims he acted alone. That he's the one with the vendetta against Ric. He said he thought he could get to him through you. Says he was pissed that Ric wouldn't sell his daughter's art at his gallery."

Ric could hear bits of the call and asked, "What's his daughter's name?"

Rob flipped the phone to speaker, so he could hear the entire call.

"Sanchez, Carmen Sanchez."

Ric thought about it and then nodded his head. "Yeah, I saw a few pieces from a Carmen Sanchez a few months back. The girl had talent, just not gallery talent."

"Well, we found several pieces of the stolen art in a back room at his place. We're questioning him about the other pieces that are still missing, including Dante's piece. It looks like we can wrap this up nice and tight. If you two want to make it on back here, we can close things out and get some more answers."

When they had gotten off the phone, Ric looked like he was deep in thought.

"What?" Rob asked him as they were packing up.

"Hmm?"

"What's that look for?" She stopped and leaned against the side of his car.

"Nothing, it's nothing."

Not buying it, she continued to look at him and crossed her arms.

"Well, it's just that it doesn't add up. You know, the missing pieces, his daughter's art. Something just doesn't feel right. If I remember correctly, Carmen Sanchez was trying to sell her art because her family was broke."

He turned and started walking around. "I turned her on to another gallery in town that might be interested in her work. I never met her father. Then there's *The Indian*, Dante Cardone's piece. Why go through all the trouble to steal that one and in the manner in which it was taken? Something just doesn't add up."

Rob thought about it and knew he was right. Something smelled funny, but until they got back to Portland and interviewed José, she didn't think they were going to find their answers.

Driving through the small town, they decided to eat

before heading back, so they stopped at The Golden Oar for lunch.

Rob finally had the chance to look at the quaint little town of Pride for the first time. The houses all sat in rows with well-maintained yards. Kids played outside on the lawns or rode bikes on the sidewalks. There were charming little stores on the main street, and they must have passed a half dozen people who all stopped and waved at Ric when they recognized him. He drove up to a large building that sat on the waterfront; it appeared to be an old warehouse that had been remodeled into the restaurant. A huge sign hung on the front of the building with the words "The Golden Oar" carved in vibrant gold letters above a large ship with white sails sitting in dark blue water.

The docks were to the left of the building and she could see boats of every variety docked there. Many of the boat slots were empty for the day, no doubt fishing boats out to get their day's catch.

"That's Jordan Shipping, Todd's business, across the street." He pointed to a four-story brick building across the way.

When they walked into the restaurant, she was greeted by a rush of warmth and wonderful smells. The entire back wall was a large wall of glass that overlooked the water, giving the guests a sense of romance and elegance.

The lighting was soft and warm, and elegant oil paintings hung on almost every wall. A large stone fireplace sat near the back of the room. The tables were lit with low candles, and the mixture of family-friendly and romance gave the place even more character.

As they were seated, she wondered if Ric had sold them any of the colorful oil paintings.

"Most of it is Iian's grandmother's work. He's added quite a few of Allison's over the last year or so." Ric smiled at her from across the table.

After they'd placed their orders, Iian walked out of the back room. He looked at home here, and they watched as he stopped and talked to several guests on his way to their table.

"I thought you two were under house arrest?" He sat easily in an empty chair next to hers. He signed as he spoke, and Rob watched him since she enjoyed trying to expand her own knowledge.

"We've been sprung," Ric said and signed along. "It sounds like they caught the guy behind all our problems. We're heading back after lunch to tie up the loose ends."

"We'll be sad to see you both go. You're welcome to come back anytime."

The dark man sat in his car and watched the couple walk into the restaurant. He knew that once José turned himself in, he'd find the whereabouts of Ric and the beautiful detective, Roberta Stanton. All he had to do was make a few calls to his friend at the phone company to trace the calls placed to Rob's cell phone. Everything was working according to his new plan.

Ric knew it was going to take him weeks to catch up on his work when he got back into town. He had a charity ball that he was supposed to hold in the next few months. He didn't mind dressing up and being wined and dined. He knew how to deal with the people that attended these kinds of events. After all, he'd been raised around them.

~

He wasn't looking forward to dealing with his mother, however, and wondered if she was still staying with Dante.

As Ric drove them out of town and hit the main road back to the highway, he couldn't help but think about his sister. He was heartbroken over her pain more than his mother's betrayal. But seeing Rob with her family had given him a little hope that maybe his family could be healed, at least a little.

Rob sat next to him in the car, deep in her own thoughts. He didn't know what was in store for them when they returned to Portland. He only knew that he wanted to continue seeing her. It had been quite some time since he'd been in a relationship. Now that his case was winding down, she had run out of excuses to not see him officially.

He'd enjoyed his time in Pride with her. Being stuck in a small place with her had been no burden at all. She was easy to talk to, easy to be with, and easy on his libido.

They were just a few miles from the turn off when a large semi came out of nowhere, hitting the side of his car. He heard Roberta scream his name, and then everything went black.

CHAPTER 19

"*R*ic, damn it, wake up." She was shaking him as blood oozed from the large gash above his left eye. His shoulder was twisted at an odd angle. She ran her hands over the rest of him, feeling for broken bones. It seemed his head and shoulder had taken the worst of the impact.

Her knee hurt, but she didn't seem to have any broken bones and there was no major bleeding. She thought she'd bumped her head, but so far her vision was fine and the pain was minimal.

She looked up and watched as the semi driver jumped out of his mangled truck into a waiting jeep and then peeled off. Making a mental note of all the details, she turned back to Ric and focused on trying to wake him. She didn't notice the man approaching the back of the car until the gun was pointing at her temple.

"Remove your weapon, Detective. Slowly," she heard him say in a thick middle-eastern accent.

She went to move her head to look at him, but he

pushed the gun against her temple a little harder and said, "Now."

Moving just her hand, she slowly released the clasp and fingered her weapon. She handed it out the shattered window to him.

"Now, if you would be so kind as to step out of the car." He reached and opened her door.

She took one last look at Ric then did as the man asked. He stood just a few inches shorter than her. His dark skin was covered by a crisp white thawb, which, with his bulk, made him look larger.

"What do you want?" She held herself stiff, ready to spring at any opening she saw. She heard Ric moan behind her, so she positioned her body, so the man wouldn't see him.

"First, I want Ric Derby dead, and then you and I are going to take a little ride." He motioned for her to step aside, but she held her ground.

"Why?" Upon his blank look, she said, "Why do you want Ric dead? What has he done to you?"

"Not to me, my dear. It's what he's done to my brother and niece. You see, he's been filling my niece's head with the idea that she could do something in life other than what her family has been planning for her since her birth."

"I don't understand." Rob could hear Ric moving around and knew that the man was now too far away to hear the slight movements.

"Sannidhi is young and impressionable. She was fooled by Ric into thinking she could actually move to America and become an artist. She'd be Americanized!" The gun wavered in his hands as he screamed.

"My brother has plans for her. She is to be a good wife

to someone of great importance. My brother Haidar had tried to keep her under control, but then a few months back she disappeared. The ticket she used to leave her family was under the name Ric Derby; he helped her escape. We think she is somewhere in Europe, alone, thanks to him. The family will find her, they are very close to locating her, but they had to explain her absence, make excuses to her promised husband, and it's all thanks to him." He pointed the gun at the empty car, and she saw his dark eyes go wide with fear.

She saw her opening then, as the man frantically searched around for Ric. She swung low as Ric came from high and behind. She heard the shot, felt the heat, but continued to kick out until Ric had the man pinned to the pavement. He continued to hit the man until he was unconscious, then he kicked the gun away.

She stood there, and then everything started moving in slow motion. She smiled down at Ric and watched the blood slowly dripping down the left side of his face as he looked at her. She could smell his blood…how funny. She could see him screaming at her, but couldn't hear him, which was even stranger. Then the world tilted and went dark.

Lights flashed as she was wheeled below even brighter lights. Ric was screaming at her again. What was he saying? She tried very hard to focus. Why was it important? She had to tell him something. She couldn't remember what it was. She saw his eyes and focused on them. Why was he crying?

$\approx$

Ric watched as they wheeled Roberta through the double doors at Edgeview Hospital. The nurse had walked him into a different area so an emergency-room doctor could take a look at his shoulder and head. His left arm hung by his side, and there was no doubt in his mind that it was dislocated. His knuckles were bloody from where he'd repeatedly hit the man who'd been holding Rob at gunpoint.

When he'd had him on the ground unconscious, he'd looked up and had seen the dark stain on Rob's chest. Ric had jumped up and grabbed Rob just before she'd slid to the ground.

The passenger van full of retired golfers, which had been the first car to come down the road, had been a blessing. One of its occupants was Aaron Steven's grandfather, a retired doctor.

He'd stood by and watched as the man and an older woman had worked on Roberta, stopping the blood that had been oozing out of her left shoulder.

When the ambulance had arrived, they'd loaded her into the back and he'd watched the local sheriff load the man who had shot her into the back of his squad car. He'd ridden in the ambulance with Rob, watching, hovering over her.

Ric looked up now as Aaron Stevens walked in.

"What happened?" Aaron asked as he rushed to his side.

"Rob, she's been shot. Can you go check on her for

me? I'm okay, just please let me know what's going on with her first," Ric pleaded.

"I'll go check and be right back." Ric watched as Aaron quickly left. Then he placed his head in his hand and prayed.

Less than ten minutes later, as a nurse was finishing cleaning his head, Aaron walked back in. The look on his face said more than his words.

"She's in surgery. Doctor Kent is the best around. He's going to take care of her. Her vitals are not good, but they aren't getting worse." Aaron walked over and started looking at Ric's shoulder. "Let's take care of this shoulder."

"I didn't know you were on staff here. I thought you had your own place."

"I do, but my grandfather called. I was in town for a meeting, so today is your lucky day. This is going to hurt," he said as he popped Ric's shoulder back into place.

Six hours later, Ric felt like he was going crazy. He was pacing up and down the small private waiting area, his arm in a sling and new stitches on the side of his head. The whole Jordan clan was there except for Lacey, who was at home watching all the young children.

Allison and Iian sat quietly huddled together. Megan and Todd had arrived shortly after them. There was even a priest, Father Michael, who was sitting talking quietly to Megan. He seemed like a nice, older gentleman.

Ric had been raised Catholic but hadn't been practicing for some time. He'd quietly prayed with the man when he'd arrived. Rob's partner, Tom, had arrived two hours after he'd let the PD know what had happened. Now there were several cops sitting around the room, as well, including her sergeant and commander.

The room was quiet, too quiet. Ric wanted answers. He walked to the door and looked out at the nurse's station. When he saw Aaron standing there, talking to another doctor, he opened the door and walked towards the men.

Rob knew what was happening; she felt herself drifting away. Everything in her head said that she was leaving, there was no pain.

Her mind flashed to a night many years ago. She was in a hotel room with her dad. He was passed out drunk on the other bed and she was staying up all night watching MTV, eating red licorice vines and Mike and Ike's, and drinking Dr. Pepper.

Then, in her mind, she was whisked away to be with her friends, months before they'd been gunned down. They were eating burgers and drinking sodas, laughing. Everyone was there—Billy, Bonnie, Tom, Jenny, and all the others, their young faces all smiling and happy.

Then she was eighteen and sitting with Detective Johns in an ice cream parlor after they'd won their case against the gang members who'd taken her friends away. They celebrated, and he asked her what her plans were for her life. His face couldn't mask the concern and friendship he felt.

Quickly, she was whisked to the small cabin with Ric. They were making love slowly after taking a walk on the beach in the summer rain. She spent more time here, realizing that it had been the happiest she'd ever been.

She watched as his face hovered above hers, his eyes filled with love. Then his eyes turned sad and tears were falling down on her as she was being wheeled down a long bright hallway. She wanted to go back to the cabin, back to the happy moment.

"Please," she begged.

"Shh, shh, it's okay, everything's going to be okay, you're safe. Just relax, rest now, I'll be here. I'll be right here," he said.

She'd been calling his name over and over from across the room. He'd woken in the uncomfortable chair he'd been sitting in for the last two days.

His friends had brought him a change of clothes, razors, whatever he had needed. Aaron had used his pull at the hospital to get Ric full access to her room, day and night. He'd showered and changed into new clothes and had stayed by her side ever since.

His friends brought him food from the hospital or the restaurant, or they made him something home cooked and brought it to him.

Roberta's friends and partners came and went. Her mother and grandmother had come and had even stayed for a few nights in a hotel nearby. Megan, Lacey, and Allison stopped by, and Todd and Iian had kept Ric company for a while. All the time, Ric had stayed, never leaving the room and only stepping into the adjoining bathroom for quick breaks.

Aaron came back every day, checking her charts and

her vitals, and checking Ric to make sure he took the medicine for his shoulder and head injuries.

Now as she stirred, Ric leaned over her and comforted her. This was the first time she'd moved since arriving at the hospital.

Her eyelids fluttered, and then she was looking at him. He could see confusion and fear.

"You're at Edgeview Hospital. You were shot." He tried to maintain his voice, but it still cracked, and he held back a sob. "The bullet was lodged less than an inch from your heart, but they got it out." He leaned down and kissed her lightly on her forehead.

When she tried to talk, he shushed her again, "Don't. They say your throat will be sore from the tubes. Everything is going to be fine, just rest. I'll be here." He watched as her eyes slid closed again.

He sat next to her and watched her sleep, her dark eyelashes resting on her pale cheeks. Over the last few days, he'd thought long and hard about losing her, about what it had done to him to see her lying on the cold ground with blood pouring from her chest and shoulder. He'd thought for a moment that he'd lost her, and it had nearly killed him.

His hands shook now as he reached over and lightly pushed a dark strand of her hair from her forehead.

He'd never felt this passionate about anyone. He couldn't think what life would be like without her; he didn't want to think about it.

Pushing up, he started to pace the room again. He swore he'd wear a pathway in the linoleum flooring soon. Just then, a nurse walked in. When she started taking Roberta's vitals, he told her that she'd briefly woken up.

"That's a good sign, Mr. Derby. I'll pass the good news along to her doctor." She quietly left the room.

Less than ten minutes later, Aaron walked in smiling.

"I heard she was awake." When Ric nodded, he continued. "Wonderful, was she coherent?"

"No, not really, she just called out."

"Well, give her some time. It's a good sign." Ric watched as Aaron double-checked her vitals and IV tubes.

"Have you had dinner?" When Ric shook his head no, Aaron said, "I can have someone bring you something. It's meatloaf night in the cafeteria. You don't want to have the meatloaf here." He shook his head. "Iian's making lasagna for the family."

"Sounds good, thank you."

After he left, Ric sat and watched Rob sleep. His phone beeped with a new message. He'd switched it to silent mode to allow Rob some quiet, and he hadn't heard it ring.

He listened to his sister's message. "Ric, it's Katie." She sounded so different, almost as if she was far away. "I heard about what happened. I just wanted you to know that I'm thinking about you and I hope Roberta gets better. I… I'm sorry I can't take your calls right now. Just know that I'm not upset with you. I just need to sort a few things out before I can deal with…everyone else. Give Rob my love. Bye."

He felt sad knowing that his perky little sister was no more. He sat in the quiet room and listened to the machines and thought about everything he'd almost lost.

Less than an hour later, there was a light knock on the door. Walking to it, he was shocked to see his father on the other side.

"Dad?" His father had the same build as Ric—lean,

tall, and toned. Ric knew his father spent as much time in the gym and running as he did. Ric's blond hair and blue eyes matched his father's perfectly. His father's hair was just shorter and neater at the moment.

Ric noticed that his pants and shirt were wrinkled, which was unusual for his father. Usually, the man's clothing was in pristine condition. He actually looked like he'd just stepped off a plane and ridden in a car for two hours, like a normal human being.

"Ric, I heard about your...detective and came as soon as possible." His father looked uncomfortable, standing in the bright hallway. Ric could see the dark circles under his eyes and could only imagine the pain the man was going through. He knew that his father had just found out that his wife of over thirty years had not only been unfaithful but had a different family and had led a separate life across the world.

"It's good to see you." Ric walked into the hallway and hugged his father.

The next day, Sergeant Johns pulled Ric out to the hallway.

"Well, it looks like Adham Rangan was the real mastermind. He's admitted to hiring the others to steal the pieces from your gallery, then trying to kill you and abduct Rob. It appears that he'd shipped several of the pieces to India for his brother, so he could recoup the loss of his daughter's dowry. Since she's still missing, he assumed you had something to do with her disappearance. Even if they had gotten her back, the shame she's caused her family is irreversible. Most likely she'll be killed if they ever find her." The sergeant shook his head. "Damn crazy country. Anyway, we recovered the pieces he hadn't shipped yet from his mansion. The man has more money than god; apparently, his family has oil money. He has a pile of lawyers fighting to get him free now. We'll see how it plays out in the courts. Most likely you'll be called in to testify."

Ric watched as the older man rubbed his hands through his hair.

"I'd like to get my hands on him myself, but he's been transferred to the state facility already. There's a possibility the feds will even get a chance at him since shipping stolen goods outside the United States is a federal and international crime. There are a lot of people piling up the charges against him."

"Thanks, Sergeant." Ric went to shake his hand.

"Please, call me Mike." He shook his hand.

"Thanks, Mike."

Roberta sat up in the bed and watched the group of grown men huddled around her. Their faces were all solemn, and she could tell they were trying to keep a positive attitude.

"Do I look that bad?" she asked Tom.

It had been three days since she'd woken up. Since then, she'd had so many visitors she couldn't count. Her mother and grandmother had driven and spent two whole days with her before they'd been assured that she was on the mend and had returned home with promises to visit her soon in Portland.

Today, it seemed, the whole Portland police department was crammed into her small hospital room, which had been filled full of amazing bouquets of flowers.

She looked around the room now for Ric, who'd been a standard feature in the room since she'd woken. She saw him standing in the corner, talking to his father, who had apparently shown up a few days ago. He hadn't left his son's side once since arriving.

He'd mentioned the wedge that had come between them, but it appeared to her that they had mended any rifts.

Ric had left her alone for only a few hours, apparently to shower and change, since he came back looking fresh in new clothes she hadn't seen yet.

She desperately wished for a shower. She'd had a nurse pull her hair up in a loose ponytail. The most she'd been allowed to do was walk to the restroom, and even then, a nurse had never left her side.

"You take your time healing. There's no rush to get back," Tom was saying.

She noticed that Sergeant Johns had not stepped forward to talk to her yet. He stuck to the back of the group and waited until everyone started to clear out. When it was just Ric, Ric's father, and the Sergeant, he stepped forward.

Rob looked at Ric and he and his father quietly walked out of the room, leaving her alone with the man who had been more of a father figure to her than her own dad had ever been.

"You scared me, little girl." He patted her hand, and

she reached up and held onto his. She'd held it together in front of the others. Now, however, she felt the tears coming.

"I scared myself." She didn't know if she could explain to this man what he'd done for her life. How could you repay someone who had saved your life in more ways than one? "Listen, Sarge." Wetting her lips, she held onto his hand. "I've never told you—"

"Shush now, you don't have to say anything." He patted her arm lightly.

"Yes, yes I do. If it wasn't for you, who knows where I would have ended up. You saw something in me that day, something no one else had ever seen. You gave me something I didn't even know I needed." Tears were slipping down her cheeks now.

"Rob, I didn't do anything that you wouldn't have done. I saw potential in a scared girl who'd just lost everything. I gave you a chance and you haven't failed me or yourself since that day. You are the strongest person I've ever known. That's why I know you're going to be back at the office doing your job as soon as you're cleared. You will continue saving and protecting others like you were born to do."

"I love you, you know that?" She smiled, then he leaned over and kissed her cheek softly.

"Yeah, I love you too, kiddo. I think there's someone else waiting to hear those words as well. Unless I'm just an old fool and have lost my ability to see the obvious." He smiled down at her and then turned and left.

CHAPTER 20

$\mathcal{L}$ ess than two weeks later, Rob sat in her living room with Jack on her lap. It felt good to be home. Apparently, when José had gone through her place, he'd torn up some of her furniture. When she'd walked in, she'd noticed the new living room couch and chairs. Her small queen bed had been replaced with a large king-sized foam mattress.

"Did you have something to do with all this?" She looked across the room at Ric who had just carried in the last of their bags from the car.

"I have no idea what you're talking about," he said with a smile.

She didn't quite know what to expect from him. Did he plan on living here with her? Would he feel comfortable in a small, modest place so unlike what he was used to?

He had no more than sat down when there was a knock on the door.

"I hope you don't mind, but while you were asleep in

the car, I ordered take out." He walked to the door expecting the deliveryman to be on the other side.

Both of them were shocked to find Dante Cardone standing there.

"Hi, I hope you don't mind me stopping by. I wanted to check up on both of you." When Rob had met him before, her impression of him had been cockiness. Now she could see that he was nervous and possibly a little scared. His eyes were searching theirs, and she realized she was wrong about him. It wasn't attitude and boldness; it was fear and nerves.

"Please." Ric stepped aside to let him in.

"I know that this is all strange to you." Dante ran his hands through his hair, something Ric also did when he was upset or nervous, and Rob noticed how much the two men had in common. Both had been raised to believe one thing and been thrown into this situation unwillingly.

"Please, come in and have a seat." Rob waved her hand towards her new leather chairs.

When they were all seated, looking at each other across the small space, Dante continued.

"Ric, I just wanted to tell you that I'm sorry I didn't come to you sooner. When I found out about you my junior year of college, I wanted to hate you. But it's been over six years now and I've grown to forgive mom...Kathleen." He looked more nervous now.

Rob sneaked a look in Ric's direction. He was sitting very straight, very stiff next to her. Reaching over, she took hold of his hand and he relaxed a little.

"I didn't know about Katie until just last year, and just now found out that she's"—he looked a little sick and sad — "she's my sister. I was led to believe that you were a mistake mom made in college, a one-night fling. Then I found out about Katie, and well, all mom's lies just weren't adding up. So I did some digging of my own. When my father opened the branch in Portland, I left school, eager to run it, to be closer. To try and understand…"

"Dante, these last few weeks, I've only been thinking about one thing—Katie. I couldn't care less that you're my half-brother. No, wait, that came out wrong. I'm happy, happy to have you and accept you. There isn't anything I can do to change the past or what our mother has done. But my main focus is the damage it has done to one of the people I care about most in this world. My…*our* little sister is the most caring, trustworthy person, I've ever met. And the fact that I haven't heard from her in almost a month scares me and pisses me off. Knowing that she is dealing with this by herself…"

"I understand. I've tried calling her myself. Mom has tried. Even my father has tried contacting her." The worry on his face matched Ric's.

"She asked me for time, and I'm trying to give it to her. I don't know you from Jack." Upon hearing his name, the cat walked over and plopped down in Ric's lap. "But I'd be happy to get to know you and give this a chance."

"I'm happy to hear that." Relief washed over Dante's face. "I've thought about this day for years. I can't tell you how happy I am to know that Mom's secret is out, that I can finally call your family."

His whole attitude changed right in front of Rob. To look at the man now, she wouldn't have pegged him the way she had just a short time ago. His concern and fear for a sister he'd never known had changed the way she looked at him, and she could tell that this was a man she'd misjudged, just as she had his brother.

~

After Dante left, they sat and ate the delivered Chinese. It wasn't as good as his old delivery place, but it would have to do.

He noticed Rob's head drooping several times and when he picked her up and carried her to bed, she held on tight and kissed his neck.

Knowing she was still weak, he tried to lay her down on the new mattress.

"No, mmm." She placed soft kisses along his jawline.

"Rob, you're killing me." He closed his eyes and just for a moment, enjoyed the featherlight kisses.

"Please, Ric. It's killing me." She tried to pull him down on the bed.

He lay down next to her and pulled her closer, "Honey, it's too soon. You're still hurting."

"I'll let you know when I'm hurting. Right now, I'm only hurting for you." She rolled over on top of him, her shoulder still held close in a sling. She sat over him and smiled, slowly pulling her arm out. He reached up and helped her remove the sling, then watched as she tossed it to the floor with a sigh.

When she reached for her shirt, he helped release the small buttons that ran up the front, going slower than he knew she wanted him to. Her eyes clouded and she rolled her head back.

Gently removing her shirt, he cupped her and let out a moan himself. He had almost forgotten what she looked and felt like. Leaning up, he put his mouth to her and remembered her taste and wanted more. He saw her fresh bandage and knew that she held her arm close to her side for comfort. Trying not to disturb her shoulder, he played his hands all over her skin until he could see small bumps rising everywhere.

When she reached to remove his shirt, he sat up and quickly removed it then pulled down her pants and his off. Then they were back on the bed, her straddling him, hovering above him. He reached up and, cupping the back of her neck, pulled her down to his mouth.

Desire so strong pounded throughout his body. He felt every muscle vibrate with want, his senses filled with her. Running his hands over her hips, he held on as she slowly rubbed herself against him.

"Please." Now he was begging her.

"What? What do you want, Ric?" she teased him.

How could she be in such control? Wasn't she burning as much as he was? Running his hands slowly towards her core, he slid his fingers under the red silk and watched as she threw her head back on a moan.

Unclasping her bra in an expert move, he freed her to his view and his mouth. Taking her into his mouth, he enjoyed the taste and slowly pushed his fingers into her slick heat at the same time.

One thing ran through his mind—he didn't want to go this long without her again.

She leaned forward and removed her panties then wrapped her fingers around him and slowly slid down until she was fully impaled on his length. When she moaned and started to move, he grabbed her hips and held on.

~

"This is bull and you know it," Ric said, pacing her small living room. "You are not ready to go in. I don't care what those doctors say."

"Ric." She waited until he turned and looked at her. "It's been almost two months. I want to get back to work. No, I *need* to go back." She was completely mended. She had a scar just below her left shoulder blade and every now and then she felt a little tightness in her arm, but other than that, she was ready.

He'd hovered over her, not allowing her to do anything or lift anything heavy since they'd been back. She was happy that he cared, but it was starting to drive her crazy.

She'd yet to say the words she'd wanted to. Somehow saying them to the sergeant was easier than saying them to Ric.

"Besides, you have that charity event in New York." She knew that he was already late leaving for the airport. "You can't expect me to stay home forever. You have your job, I have mine." She tucked her shirt in and strapped on her gun. She'd missed the weight of it. "Besides, you know the sergeant. Do you honestly think he's going to let me do anything more than pushing a stack of papers around until he makes sure I'm ready?"

Ric looked concerned, his forehead squashed in concentration. "Fine, I know you're right."

She left the room and he followed, stopping to pick up his bag, which was sitting by the front door. She turned. "Go, you're already late. You know how the airports are now that you have to strip naked upon command," she joked.

Fifteen minutes later, she pulled into the parking garage at the station and almost had a panic attack. Closing her eyes, she tried to breathe slowly.

What was wrong with her? Resting her head on the steering wheel, she closed her eyes.

It had been so close. What would she have done if it had been Ric that had been shot? That thought had crossed her mind for the past few weeks. Now she was sending him to New York for almost a week. What would she do if he didn't return?

Images flashed through her mind of them on the beach together, or in the kitchen making dinner, making love in the shower or the bedroom...

Making up her mind, she turned on her car, placed her lights on the roof, bolted from the parking garage, and got on her phone.

"Am I on some sort of watch list?" Ric had had enough. He'd been pulled out of the line for the third time to be searched. He held his shoes in his hands while his wallet and briefcase were being searched for the second time. The damn wand hadn't even beeped when, for the tenth time, someone ran it over every inch of him.

"This is harassment. I mean, how many times can you search a man?" Just then, he heard the last call for his flight. "Great, now I've missed my—"

"Is there a problem here?" He heard a sexy voice behind him and spun around.

"You? You did this?" He dropped his shoes.

"I had to stall you. You were leaving before I could tell

you something." He tried to pull her over, out of the main section, where there were at least a hundred-people watching them. She stopped him.

"Ric Derby, would you do me the honor of marrying me?" She said in a loud clear voice, which caused many more people to look in their direction, laughing and cheering.

He stood there and looked at her like he'd been hit over the head.

"I love you and I think that you…" She chewed her bottom lip.

"Of course, I love you," he interrupted, looking relieved.

Smiling, she continued. "Make an honest woman out of me and marry me."

"Isn't this kind of backward?" he asked, looking around at all the faces of the people waiting to hear his answer. Everyone stood there holding their breath, totally involved in his private affairs. He could see fear starting to show in Rob's eyes.

"I want nothing more in my life than to be married to a hot-headed detective with bedroom eyes. Yes, of course, I'll marry you, Roberta Stanton." He pulled her close and kissed her to the cheers of everyone around them.

"*Y*ou know, you could have chosen anywhere to go for our honeymoon." Ric pulled her closer.

"I know. I married a millionaire who could fly me to the ends of the earth and back." She looked over her shoulder and smiled at him. "But I still prefer staying here."

They stood on the deck of the small cabin and looked out at the ocean as the sun was setting. The colors were something she'd never forget. Never wanted to forget.

This small cabin was her happy place. So naturally, when he told her to pick where she wanted to go, she'd chosen the one place she'd been the happiest.

The small town of Pride had not only grown on her, she believed they belonged here, together.

"Well, this time next year we should be in our own place." He kissed the top of her head.

He'd surprised her with an early wedding present, the title to ten acres just down the road from where they now stood. The beachfront property was beautiful; they'd picked the house plans out together. By the time they'd officially been married, the foundation had already been poured.

Now she just needed to convince Ric to spend more than half a year there.

She'd quietly resigned from the department. It had taken some convincing, but she'd gotten a lucrative offer from a private company to oversee their security, and she just couldn't turn it or him down.

After all, who would be better to protect his business than an ex-thief?

SERVING PRIDE – SNEAK PEEK

*L*ittle Robert listened to his mom crying in the next room. He knew that he couldn't go in there yet. He had to wait until Roy left before he could go see how bad the damage was from the fight. Chances were Roy would either pass out drunk within fifteen minutes or he'd grab his keys and leave, heading down to the local bar to get even more wasted.

It was a hell of a way to spend his eighth birthday. He had enjoyed the party earlier; all of his friends had attended, and he'd gotten loads of cool presents. But shortly after the last guest had left, Roy had started drinking. It had taken less than an hour for his mother to do or say something that had caused the fight. Robert knew it wasn't her fault.

He could remember a time when his mother had been pretty and strong. Back when his real father, Robert Sr., had been alive, she'd smiled and laughed a lot. But when he was six, his dad had died in a car accident and his mother stopped living.

She hadn't started dating until just last year, and the first person she'd picked was Roy. She'd met him at the bar where she worked six nights a week. At first, Roy had smiled and brought presents for them. Shortly after he moved into their small two-bedroom apartment, the fights began. Robert didn't know why his mother kept him around, why she allowed him to still live there. There really wasn't anything the man was good for. After all, shortly before he'd moved in, he'd lost his job at the steel mill.

Robert didn't like him not only because of this but also because the man called him Robby, which he couldn't stand. He always used a tone, like he was making fun of him or that he had a secret joke somehow tied up in his nickname. But his mother acted like she loved him, and so Robert had tolerated him.

Plus, Roy had promised them both that he'd find a new job and take care of them. But then he'd started drinking. Robert even thought that he was using drugs, though he couldn't really tell. He never took drugs in front of him, but Robert had listened carefully to the police officer who had talked to his class when his school had a drug awareness week. The man had spoken about saying no to drugs but hadn't really talked about how to tell if someone else was on drugs.

After the officer's planned speech was done, Robert had walked up to him and asked him how to tell if someone else was on drugs. The man had looked at him funny, and then he sat down and talked to him, giving Robert a few things, he should look out for. He asked Robert if he was okay and tried to get him to tell him who

Robert thought was on drugs. But Robert didn't want to get Roy, or worse, his mother, in any trouble, so he'd just told the man that there were some kids that bugged him on his walk home.

He'd enjoyed talking to the officer and had eyed the man's gun like it was candy. He knew guns were dangerous and needed to be handled by professionals, but man, he really wanted to see how much it weighed and feel how it felt in his hands. Maybe someday he'd get to hold a real gun and even fire it.

Now he listened to Roy leave, then waited a few more minutes before he crawled out of his bed with his Spider-man comforter and sheets. As he tip-toed down the short hall, he listened for the front door, just in case, Roy decided to come back. If he did, Robert would make a bolt for his room. Roy had never hit him, probably because if he ever laid a hand on him, his mama will the man. She'd said so on many occasions.

"Mama?" He pushed the door opened and looked into the dark room. He could just make out his mother on the bed in the dark room.

"Go back to bed, honey." He heard her sniffle and she quickly rolled over, putting her back to him.

He walked over to the other side of the bed and looked at her. "Mama, are you okay? Should I call the police?"

"No, honey. We just had a fight. Roy's just stressed that he hasn't found a job yet."

"Mama, did he hit you?" Robert had been asleep for the first part of the fight. All the sugar and running around during his party had worn him out. He'd actually gone to bed an hour earlier than normal.

"No, baby. He just yelled." His mother sat up and turned on the light. Robert saw that her eyes were swollen red from crying. She still had on the dress that she'd worn for his party. It was her happy dress, as Robert liked to think of it. The pale yellow reminded him of better times with his father, for some reason.

She patted the mattress next to her and he climbed up next to her on the bed. When she wrapped her arm around him, he felt comforted. He loved the way his mother smelled, as fresh as a field of daisies. That's what his father had always said, and Robert had always agreed with him.

"I'm sorry to wake you. Did you have fun today?"

Being the eight-year-old boy that he was, he fell for the change of subject his mother provided and proceeded to talk for a few minutes about his party and all the cool presents he'd gotten that day. He fell asleep again, there in her arms, and she carried him back to his room and sung to him as she laid him back in his Spider-man bed.

The next morning when he woke, she was gone. There was no note, no goodbyes, nothing. Roy had come back and had fallen asleep on the couch, face down. When Robert tried to wake him, he'd just turned over and put the pillow over his head.

Robert thought that maybe his mom had gone to the store, so he got ready for school. He made his own lunch and grabbed a few slices of bread and some cheese for breakfast. Roy didn't move, even though Robert was being very loud in the kitchen.

When he left to walk for school, his mother still wasn't there. Leaving the apartment complex, he saw by his mother's car still parked in the parking lot, and for a second, he wanted to run back in the apartment to see if maybe she had just been hiding from him. She couldn't have gone anywhere without her car. He thought that maybe she'd taken Roy's truck, but when he looked, he saw that it was parked out back behind the apartments.

It took him twice as long, as usual, to walk to school that day because he was so occupied by his thoughts. When he finally did make it to class, he was fifteen minutes late and received his third tardy that year.

Walking home with a note that needed to be signed, he stepped in to find Roy still on the couch face down. He'd forgotten to check and see if his mother's car was there, but he knew instantly that she wasn't home. She was supposed to work until midnight that night since she'd taken off the day before for his birthday party.

Walking into his room, he dumped his bag on his bed and got to work on his homework. He had an agreement with his mom. If he kept his grades above C's he would get to play Xbox after dinner. Since his mother was at work, he could eat dinner as early as he wanted, which meant more time for playing games.

That whole evening, Roy didn't move. He'd walked by him several times to make sure he was still breathing and was slightly disappointed when he heard the man snoring.

The next morning, he rushed into his mom's room to find it empty. Roy was no longer on the couch. When he got home from school, neither of them were there. Since it was Friday, he called for pizza delivery and paid out of the money his mom hid for him. He spent the weekend playing video games and eating junk food.

When he went into school on Monday, he still hadn't heard from either his mom or Roy. Instead of going to his class, he'd walked into the principal's office and sat out by the receptionist. He told the older woman he needed to speak with Mr. Kent, man to man, before classes.

Finally, a few minutes later, Mr. Kent walked out and nodded to him to follow him into his office.

"Well, Mr. Brogan, what can I help you with today?"

Robert sat in the large leather chair and looked across at the principal.

"Well sir, I think something happened to my mom and Roy."

Instantly the man's face showed concern. "What do you mean?"

"I haven't seen my mom since last week and Roy took off, too. It's not like my mom to leave this long. Her work called and left a message, saying she was fired. Roy, well, Roy doesn't work, and his truck has been gone for a few days."

"Who's been watching you?"

"No one, sir. I've been on my own since the day after my birthday." Robert hadn't realized tears were escaping his eyes and when a fat drop landed on his hand, he jumped and looked down at it like it had fallen from out of nowhere.

Mr. Kent picked up his phone, "Mary, can you call Child Protective Services, please. Tell them it's an emergency."

Robert can't really remember what took place in the days that followed, but less than a week later, he was on a plane to someplace called Oregon. He was going to live with his great-aunt by the ocean. He'd never seen the ocean and the excitement almost won out over the fear.

When they told him that they thought his mother had abandoned him, he screamed and kicked until they finally agreed that maybe something had happened to her. They hadn't found Roy or his mother's car or Roy's truck. Since he'd never known Roy's last name, something young kids don't think of remembering, and since the man wasn't on the lease, they didn't even know where to start looking.

Stepping off the plane, the first thing he noticed was that it was cold. New Mexico was always warm. Then he saw snow on the ground and his fear turned into excitement.

There was an older woman sitting in a wheelchair with a handmade sign that had his name on it in bright red and blue letters. Red and blue were his favorite colors. He saw this as a good sign.

Walking up to her, he dropped the hand of the stewardess who'd accompanied him on his flight. "I'm Robert Brogan. Are you my aunt Daisy?"

She leaned over and smiled at him. "Yes, sir, I am. I'd recognize you anywhere. You look just like your daddy."

The drive from the Portland airport to the town of Pride seemed to take forever. He didn't quite know what to say to his aunt. He found her car totally fascinating, though. He found her car totally fascinating She had it fitted with special controls, so she could use her hands to work the gas and brake pedals. At first, he'd been afraid of how she was going to get in the car. He'd wanted to ask if she needed any help, but she'd quickly hopped into her seat like she was a professional. What took her the longest was getting her wheelchair folded up and put in the seat behind her. He could have helped, but he was afraid he'd upset her.

"Well, Robert, I don't know what they told you, but I was your father's aunt. We were very close when he was younger, but when he moved down south, I guess we lost track of each other. I hadn't heard any news about him until he passed away." She looked over at him as she drove. "I hope you don't mind cats. I have a few of them. They make me feel better. I bet you're dying to ask me what happened to my legs, huh?"

He nodded his head in agreement and she laughed. She looked younger when she laughed, and he couldn't help but smile back at her.

"Well, a while back, I had a stroke, and since then, my legs just won't follow what my brain tells them to do. Don't worry, the rest of me seems to be working just fine and since the doctor started giving me some new medicine, I've never felt better." She smiled at him again.

"Let's see, you're in the second grade?"

He nodded his head in agreement, again.

"Good, I think I've gotten everything set up for you to start school next week. I hope it's okay that I decided to let you have the rest of this week off. I don't think you'll miss that much. Besides, we'll have fun getting to know each other."

"I'm just staying here until my mom comes back." He wanted to shout it. He'd told the CPS worker over and over again that he wanted to stay at home. He was sure that his mom was going to come home and if he wasn't there, he was worried she would think that something bad had happened to him.

"It's okay, honey, we'll wait for her together. I'm sure

she'll come back for you. You can just stay with me until she does. Will that be okay?"

This was the first person who'd actually believed him about his mother. Hearing her words made him finally believe that his mother wasn't coming back, that she couldn't come back for him, and he had a sinking feeling he knew why.

This is a work of fiction. Names, characters, places and incidents either are the product of the author's imagination or are used fictitiously, and any resemblance to actual persons, living or dead, business establishments, events or locales is entirely coincidental.

LASTING PRIDE

DIGITAL ISBN: 978-1-942896-22-7

PRINT ISBN: 9781490909264

Copyright © 2013 Jill Sanders

Copyeditor: Erica Ellis – inkdeepediting.com

Entangled Series – Paranormal Romance

The Awakening

The Beckoning

The Ascension

Haven, Montana Series

Closer to You

Never Let Go

Holding On

Pride Oregon Series

A Dash of Love

My Kind of Love

Season of Love

Tis the Season

Dare to Love

Where I Belong

Wildflowers Series

Summer Nights

Summer Heat

Stand Alone Books

Twisted Rock

For a complete list of books:

http://JillSanders.com

ABOUT THE AUTHOR

Jill Sanders is a New York Times, USA Today, and international bestselling author of Sweet Contemporary Romance, Romantic Suspense, Western Romance, and Paranormal Romance novels. With over 55 books in eleven series, translations into several different languages, and audiobooks there's plenty to choose from. Look for Jill's bestselling stories wherever romance books are sold or visit her at jillsanders.com

Jill comes from a large family with six siblings, including an identical twin. She was raised in the Pacific Northwest and later relocated to Colorado for college and a successful IT career before discovering her talent for writing sweet and sexy page-turners. After Colorado, she decided to move south, living in Texas and now making her home along the Emerald Coast of Florida. You will find that the settings of several of her series are inspired by her time spent living in these areas. She has two sons and off-set the testosterone in her house by adopting three furry little ladies that provide her company while she's locked in her writing cave. She enjoys heading to the beach, hiking, swimming, wine-tasting, and pickleball with her husband, and of course writing. If you have read any of her books, you may also notice that there is a love of food, especially sweets! She has been blamed for a few added pounds by her assistant, editor, and fans... donuts or pie anyone?

facebook.com/JillSandersBooks

twitter.com/JillMSanders

bookbub.com/authors/jill-sanders

Made in the USA
Coppell, TX
12 July 2022

79888569R00128